Of Water & Wine

a novel

<u>Of Water & Wine</u>

a novel

Robert Bell

B **B** HEME PRESS

Edited by Lori McLellan

Text and page design by magpie media/Patricia Cipolla

Lines appearing on page 46 are from Hymn 537 of the
Presbyterian Church's Book of Praise (Copyright © 1972).
Originally titled "Light's abode, celestial Salem," the words
are by St. Thomas a Kempis and translated by John Mason
Neale.

Canadian Cataloguing in Publication Data

Bell, Robert, 1971-
Of water and wine: a novel

ISBN 1-894498-12-7

I. Title.

PS8553.E456383O3 2001   C813'.6   C2001-930369-6
PR9199.3.B377383O3 2001

First published in 2001

Printed and bound in Canada

Boheme Press
110 Elena Crescent, Suite 100B
Maple, Ontario, Canada L6A 2J1
www.bohemeonline.com

for sara

Acknowledgments

This book could not have been written without the help of many people, to them I wish to express my sincerest thanks:

To my wife, Sara, who read and believed.

To my parents, Kathy and Marc, for their unwavering belief in their sons.

To Max Maccari, my publisher, and Lori McLellan, my editor, who made this a better book.

To Matt Bin, John Ferns, Wendy Morgan, Nancy Vanderzwan and all those who offered their insight, encouragement, and guidance.

To Timothy Findley, Joe Kertes, and all those at the Humber School for Writers—a program which is grooming a generation of authors.

To my grandparents, Albra Outhet and Roy MacDonald, who believed the past was valuable enough to be remembered.

And to DLG, you already know why.

R.B.

one

It was the summer of 1916, that precarious year. It was a year of things gone wrong, the unflinching hand of misfortune touching each family in its own way. Throughout the world, the old empires had begun to wince at the butchery in which their vanity had trapped them. But instead of curbing disaster, they swam farther into the current, drawing millions after them. Such are the drowning, whose grip is stronger than the whole world.

That summer, the trains winding through the forests of Ontario's north carried one of two things: soldiers or tourists. The former headed east toward Europe, while the latter went in the opposite direction just as fast as they could.

Heading into the hills and trees, soldiers hung out windows to watch the trains of tourists that passed them. Blinking into the sun, each man was enveloped by the ownerless trace of perfume, the jealous echo of chastity and sane existence among all the smoke and clatter. Fragments of a world fast disappearing.

Sitting back in her seat, Albra Creighton watched as her

brother Paul played with his Sunday collar. Hannah, their mother, had insisted they travel in their best clothes. An hour after leaving Union Station, all five of her children were reduced to distraction and misery. For Albra, this was only compounded by the humiliation of being dressed in blue to match her brother. Though they barely touched on the seat they shared, she felt it—his claim on her, not as her brother, but as a twin. The burden of that word. An umbilical millstone.

Across the aisle, the oldest child, Edward, sat rocking to the sway of the train. At seventeen Eddie stood as tall as his father, still hanging in that awkward tension between youth and manhood. Squeezed beside him were his sisters Elizabeth and Laura, both trying to relieve their boredom by reading a magazine together. In their mid-teens, they were still good companions, though the two could not have been more dissimilar in person. The older of the two, Elizabeth, had inherited her father's quiet and brooding demeanour. However, like her sister, Elizabeth was good-natured and even playful, though she lacked the confidence and early sense of sexuality which had already pointed Laura out as a beauty.

Hannah had last heard that term in her own youth, and it brought now a sense of assurance that she lacked in adult life. When her doubts became too much she would watch Laura, noting the unchecked energy of her daughter's eyes until her own were glazed with something close to envy.

The train cleaved through a town, dirty children waving as they passed. Farms and roads slipped by outside their window.

"So hot," Paul complained.

"There, there," Hannah scolded. "There, there."

Most of the family was asleep within a few hours of leaving Union Station. Beside Albra, her brother slept with his head resting on their mother's breast. Like neglected dolls her sisters sat propped against one another, awash in a slumber of pink organdie. Across the aisle their father dozed, his hand resting on a dog-eared copy of Homer. Calvin Creighton made a habit of reading the book to his family, passing on in his own way the notions closest to him.

Sighing quietly, Albra resigned herself to looking out the window. They had travelled for hours through endless forest, the train carving its way through hills of virgin rock. Interspersed between lakes the oily smudge of lumber camps passed before their window. Shirtless men stood watching the train. Behind them a blue haze of smoke hovered above the trees.

Then, as the train wound into the hills, Albra caught sight of a narrow strip of beach freckled with boats. Behind it all stood a three-storeyed building painted white against the horizon of pine and spruce.

"Wake up," she whispered. "We're here."

For those with financial mobility, the Highland Inn was a bastion of civilized comforts amid the fierce beauty of the north. Flanked by stands of pine on a rise of ancient granite, the Inn was a sanctuary of tennis courts, a dance hall and grand piano, French wines and hot baths. Strolling through the Highland's lobby, one was as likely to overhear tips for choosing stocks as those for lures. Third and fourth-generation Canadians, most guests here pursued interests inherited from their grandfathers.

Yet if these were the Dominion's monied elite, the guests of the Highland also shared an interest in that vast glimpse of wilderness that is their country. Still beyond the reach of most Prohibitionists, one could sip Scotch here on the hotel verandah and look out over the border of civilization.

After seeing to their bags, Calvin followed the concierge

up the broad pine staircase to their rooms. Still agitated from the trip, Hannah padded about hanging clothes while Calvin sat by the window with a cigar.

When she was finished, Hannah sat back roughly on the bed. "I wish you would save that for outside."

"Of course. Only we just arrived."

"The linen will hold the odour."

"Then I'll leave the window open."

"What, and risk a draft?"

The dining room was almost full as they came down to dinner where waiters moved with choreographed ease among the constellation of guests. The family was quite tired from the journey and ate mostly in silence. Only Eddie talked, leaning over the back of his chair to ask a boy named Jack Elliott about the fishing.

As they drank their tea, Calvin seemed to rouse himself. Sitting up, he passed his hand over each cheek hesitantly.

"After dinner I'll look into acquiring a boat."

Eddie nodded. "Saw some as we came in."

Calvin turned to his youngest son. "Shall we have a look after dinner?"

Paul frowned.

"You know he hates the water," said Hannah.

Calvin smiled, glancing at the other tables. "But that's where the fish are."

Eddie examined his brother with disapproval. "Besides, you'll be in the boat."

"That doesn't matter."

"Why not come down to the dock this evening?" Calvin tried again. "You can help me pick out a canoe."

There was an uncomfortable silence, after which Paul shook his head resolutely. Albra stared at her stubby row of fingers, like ribs against the bleached white of the table cloth.

"No, of course not."

Calvin paused to light a cigar, shaking out the match as he stood.

Hannah fanned at the smoke languidly. "Please, Calvin . . ."

"Not to worry," he remarked, then turned and left.

That evening Paul went to bed early with his mother where she read his favourite childhood story. The significance of the book was not lost on his sister, however, who refused to follow. As a child she would listen before bed to her mother's reading voice, sugared and indulgent, wishing Gretel would push them both into the oven.

Only much later that night did she crawl sulkily into the bed she shared with Paul. Though tired, Albra could not sleep, and for a long time she lay listening in the dark. She was confused by what she felt; she had not realized how much she wanted what Paul had been offered until her brother had refused it. Why, she wondered, was he so reluctant to join their father? Didn't he know what it meant? The sound of voices slowly faded outside and soon there came the calm murmur of wind. A loon's distant laugh rose from among the hills.

Albra woke up towards dawn. From behind the door came the hushed sound of her father's voice, drifting into the room and under her bed like leaves. Closing her eyes she turned back to the soft drone of Paul's breathing. Outside the lake reflected back the sun's first rays.

That morning, they sat out on the large chairs with the blueberries Elizabeth had picked with her mother. From the lake a slight breeze tugged at the quiet flowers on Hannah's skirt, offering flight. Paul was not feeling well after breakfast so Hannah had gathered the twins about her while Elizabeth and Laura went down to the lake.

Hannah sat with her legs trapped beneath her, watching Laura in her white dress as she flirted with the lifeguard. The breeze had caught Laura's hair, and the boy was helping to untangle it from the brooch she wore. Hannah almost smiled

to see how easily she did it, at the same time remembering . . .
Then quite suddenly, Hannah stood and began waving to
Elizabeth and Laura.

"Come back!"

In a minute Laura was standing beside her mother, holding one shoe in each hand.

"Let's take the twins for a walk along the shore."

"Shall we?"

"Yes, let's."

Laura glanced down at her sister. "Are you going to eat all
the berries?"

Looking up from the bowl, Albra ran a purple tongue of
affirmation across her lips.

Hannah smiled quietly at the twins. "My little couple. You
look so splendid together."

Laura bent down to collect her hat. "Just like Adam and
Eve," she trilled.

Albra scowled to herself.

Half an hour later, with towels and bathing suits, they followed the railway along the shore. Elizabeth led the way, holding Paul's hand as he tried to balance along the rail. Behind
came Hannah, who talked quietly with Laura. Hanging on to
her mother's skirt, Albra made a game of stepping only on the
railway ties.

Around the first bend they came to a bridge which
spanned a brief marsh and behind it a narrowing river. Sitting
on a point of rock, Hannah watched her children as they swam.

Kneeling beside his mother, Paul began dropping stones
into the water, watching wide-eyed as they disappeared into
the lake. He kept this up for some time until his mother sent
him off to find his sister. Hannah sat alone, looking over her
children. Laura, she saw, swam well, her legs sinuous and pale
beneath the water. Then, noting an absence, she stood to locate
the twins.

Paul and Albra looked up instinctively at the sound of their mother's voice. Her words came lazily, elongated by the summer heat and barely audible among the reeds and mud where they squatted.

Paul waded off in search of their mother.

Let him go, Albra thought.

She sat down in the mud again. But after squishing about some more she quickly noticed her enjoyment had become hollow. It was no longer fun without Paul. Albra resented her brother for things like this, yet loved him too with the dogged endurance of an arranged marriage. She did not understand this claim he had on her, only that it restrained her, holding her back from something for which she still had no words.

Sulking, Albra waded out of the reeds and into the water. As her feet left the ground, she stretched out across the surface of the lake, trusting the water to carry her.

Seeing Albra, Elizabeth and Laura swam out to join her. But halfway out they stopped suddenly, jerking their heads toward the shore.

"What's that?" Elizabeth whispered.

Albra paused to watch the train as it emerged in full view. Like a giant cyclops, she thought, remembering her father. Out of the windows hung the arms and faces of new recruits, each pink with the anxieties of virginity and war.

Wrinkling her nose from the soot, Albra climbed up the bank toward the passing train. From the lake Laura and Elizabeth waved with both hands at the dark cars of soldiers.

"So much whistling," they remarked.

Her mother stood up, brushing the dust from her skirt. "It's only some soldiers' song."

Albra laughed, tilting her head slightly to watch the light glancing off the water.

The engine reached the end of the lake now, letting out a whistle before turning away along the shore. Shielding her eyes again, she gazed at the heavy exhaust of smoke lurking about the trees.

Thirty years later she would sit on that bridge next to where her mother, long since dead, now stood. Balancing her canvas on the abandoned trellis, she would paint this scene almost exactly as she saw it now. For this moment, however, Albra was content to watch as the black tail of smoke faded among the trees.

Farther down the shore, the engine let out a final cry and the train began to speed up.

Still waving, Albra stopped as something beneath a passing car caught her eye. Its identity was almost lost in the thundering rush of steel and dust, and her first thought was that it might be an animal or piece of debris caught up by the train. But at the last moment there was a flash of recognition: a face— the mouth wrenched open as if to cry out, its eyes meeting Albra's for an instant. And then it was gone.

"Oh my God," Albra whispered.

They ate lunch that day under large canopies on the back lawn while the constable from town dealt with the body. Before going in, Albra had sneaked out to watch them through the railing. A circle of men gathered about the cart that had come back with the body. Albra could not take her eyes off the two large gunny sacks as each was lifted into the back of a truck. The constable stood to the side, one hand resting on his revolver.

A sombre mood hung among the guests that afternoon. Men sat in stalwart silence, dutifully listening while their wives leaked whispers of distress. Beside Hannah and her children sat a woman who sipped gin from one hand while eating delicate-looking sandwiches with the other. In want of distraction, she turned to Hannah as soon as she was seated.

"Of course you know why they have us eating back here?" An avid publicist of catastrophe, the woman was yearning to discuss the morning's excitement.

"But you weren't there were you? She was such a young woman. A girl, really. It would be cruel to call her heavy, but so charming she made up for it. Used to wait on Bertrand and me in the evening. Sweet, and so free of city airs. More's the pity . . ."

The girl she spoke of was an employee of the Highland named Irene Boyd. They found her legs almost on top of the silver tray she had been carrying. The rest of her body was dragged over three miles, out of sight for all but the most athletic mourners.

That evening, Albra leaned against the verandah railing watching her father blow cigar smoke out toward the lake. He was reclining in one of the mammoth wooden chairs that usually sat down by the dock. She stood aside for the waiter who brought him brandy in a glass wider than her hand.

Following the cigar to his mouth, she watched the tip's vehement glow. A breeze came from the east and she shivered as the smoke disappeared into the dark.

"Did you have a nice day?"

She almost jumped at this sudden break in the silence. Her index finger began winding around a stray piece of thread from her dress.

"We saw a train."

Calvin frowned. "Yes, I heard."

Albra stood quietly.

"What did you think of it?"

She stepped back from him to think. "It reminded me of the Cyclops."

Calvin turned in the chair to look at his child. He was pleased and probably surprised. Her eyes were as green as his own, and he almost smiled to recognize the stare she returned.

"Do you like trains?"

"They look like a cyclops," she repeated.

He tossed the cigar negligently over the railing. From somewhere inside the hotel came a muffled clatter of dishes, which reverberated softly on the other side of the lake. Reaching out with her left hand, Albra brought her palm to rest on his heavy brown knuckles.

"Tomorrow I want to go in the boat," she whispered, afraid now. Don't leave me here, she wanted to add, remembering the girl beneath the train.

Calvin shifted quietly in his chair. "We'll pack a lunch," he murmured.

☙

The next morning, the hotel was still asleep when Calvin woke her. Rubbing her eyes, Albra stepped from the drugged luxury of sleep onto the cool pine floor. Paul stirred just as she finished lacing her shoes. His voice sounded high and anxious.

"Where are you going?"

Albra put her finger to her mouth. "You'll wake Mother."

"Where?" he whispered.

"Fishing."

Paul rubbed his eyes stiffly. "Will you come with us this afternoon?"

"No. We're taking lunch." And it was then, feeling Paul panic, that a wave of something close to relief washed over her. Albra realized that she had unexpectedly stepped beyond her brother's reach.

"You said you'd teach me to swim." His voice sounded whiny, like Laura's when she spoke to the lifeguard.

"Mother will go with you."

Shutting the door on him, she felt a jab of regret. She could picture him holding their mother's hand as he inched toward the end of the dock. Both of them hanging over the edge, looking down.

Leaning over the gunnel, Albra studied her reflection in the lake. She sat between her father and Eddie, her back cramped against the basket carrying their lunch. Not being able to paddle, she was afforded an undisturbed view of the trees. For miles she traced the tangled knots of tree and rock which stretched back through shadows into the hills. From the face of bare granite clung full-grown balsam, each one poised effortlessly like birds on an elephant's back. If she squinted, Albra could make a single tree disappear within the thicket, fading into sloping curves of green, each hill interwoven with others, a tapestry with one thread.

Leaning back again, she watched her brother paddle. He had grown almost a foot in the last two years and his frame was only now catching up.

"Might be clearing." Eddie pointed to a patch of sun off to the east.

Calvin was quiet.

"We going to stop soon?"

"It's not even ten, boy."

From where she sat, she could see Eddie's shoulders twitch.

"Maybe in an hour or two."

They paddled in silence.

Closer to noon, Calvin drew the canoe along side of a likely-looking point. As Eddie tied up the boat, Albra leaned forward and grabbed the basket.

"Where will we eat?"

Eddie shrugged.

Their father came up behind them. "Looks like a good

view from there," pointing to a shelf of rock thirty or forty yards behind them.

Eddie looked hopefully at his sister. "You gonna carry that?"

"Yep."

Calvin headed into the brush. "Let's go then."

Holding the basket in front of her, Albra used it to push through the scrub and lower branches, following her father and Eddie up a steep incline. They were waiting for her at the top.

Eddie turned to his father. "She's being a sport."

Albra came over and sat heavily beside them.

Calvin glanced down at his daughter. "It's farther than it looks."

"You were right," she puffed. "Good view."

Calvin handed out sandwiches wrapped in wax paper. Their perch looked east over the lake. Eddie ate quickly, gulping down his lunch in large mouthfuls.

The sun broke in patches through the clouds, skipping off the lake in shards of silver. Surrounding everything was the groan of wind dragging through the branches above them.

Calvin paused, cupping his hands against the breeze to light a cigar. It caught and he drew heavily. Thick twists of smoke emerged from the sides of his mouth like a thought taking shape.

"We come for these rocks that are older than our names for them," he said eventually. "They measure the erosion of eternity. Our only consolation is that we cannot help but perish first . . ."

Albra glanced at Eddie but he was staring at their father. Calvin was given to pontifical outbursts and though it embarrassed his children, they were equally awed by his sense of grandeur. Albra looked at her father between bites of apple. It would be like this, she thought. I knew it.

Later that afternoon they paddled on the east side of the shore, soaking in the August sun that sat above the hills. Rounding a point, they turned into a small bay that narrowed to a vein of marsh and bone-white stumps. Calvin drew the canoe close to shore. "Wonder where that goes . . . ?"

Taking his cue, Eddie stood up in the bow to see. "Hard to tell," he reported. "Creek curves off into the bush. I bet there's good fishing there."

"Alright, sit down."

"Wanna look?"

Albra turned to see her father shake his head. "Too late for that."

"Tomorrow then?" Eddie liked new holes.

Calvin just stared. "It's a long way to come for such a small spot."

Eddie turned to his sister. "How 'bout it, Al?"

She nodded. "I think we should."

Their father turned the canoe back toward the open water. "Some other time."

Turning his head, Eddie spit quietly into the lake.

For the next week, Albra was woken before light by either Eddie or her father. Setting out in the sanction of dawn, they never travelled farther than half a day's paddle. Yet what Albra saw of the hills' ominous virginity jarred the compliance and monotony of her life.

ૹ

During the second week of their vacation, Calvin decided to explore the hidden estuary they had seen that first day Albra came fishing with them. There had been a heavy dew that morning and she sat with a wet bottom, grudgingly thankful for the sweater her mother had forced her to take. Each morning now Hannah met her on the way down to the dock. In the lightless dawn, she inspected Albra before releasing the girl to her father.

"Do you have the sweater I laid out?"

"Mh-hm."

"Do you?"

"Yes."

"Alright then." Hannah kissed her forehead. "Have a nice time."

She turned away, ducking her mother's embrace. "I always do."

If this sort of casual cruelty surprised Hannah, she was not alone. Albra, too, was stunned by her own callousness. Until now she had spent her life largely under her mother's gaze, having little to do with her father. But in Paul's abdication of his place on those fishing trips, an unexpected opening had formed in their father's world. Albra had filled it instinctively, sensing an opportunity to separate herself from Paul and their mother. And so each morning now she woke with a terrible sense of anticipation, as though she was about to do something very wrong.

From where she sat in the canoe, Albra watched the opalescent sliver in the horizon. She shivered, tucking each foot beneath her. Along the shore, a fallen tree shone ghostly white in the dim morning glow, like the skeleton of some prehistoric creature. As they rounded the first point, Albra looked back to see the hotel completely enveloped in mist.

An hour later Eddie cited the clusters of reeds that nearly concealed the river's entrance. He held his paddle up like a compass. "Over there."

"I see it."

The canoe slowed to pass among the tangle of stumps which littered the river mouth. Beyond this the estuary narrowed until, reaching the top of the river, they emerged into open water again. It was not a wide lake, though at the far end

Albra could see a clearing where fire had stripped the hills, which now stood exposed and charred.

"Fire," Eddie mused, speaking in the past tense.

Calvin shielded his eyes. "Looks like."

"Take a look?"

"Could."

"What do you say, Al?"

Albra leaned over the gunnel to see past her brother. "Sure."

Eddie lowered his head. "Alright, then."

Half-way up the lake they were stopped by a loud clap which came from the shore.

Albra jerked up on her knees. "What was that?"

Eddie's paddle paused in mid-stroke.

"Gun shot." Calvin stopped paddling to shield his eyes again.

"See anyone?"

"Not yet."

"Where'd it come from?"

There was another pause as each of them scanned the scorched shoreline. Another clap, and Eddie almost stood in excitement.

"There!" he yelled, gesturing toward a blunt point of scrub. Another shot reverberated across the lake. Above the underbrush they could see the tops of hats lurching toward the point.

Through the charred branches crashed a black bear and her cub, followed immediately by the pursuing men. The animals' momentum pushed them almost into the water before they could turn to find another route. But by then it was too late.

Eddie leaned forward, his paddle creaking under his weight.

A loose ring of bodies emerged from the brush. Almost as

soon as she turned on them the adult bear was knocked to the ground by two rifles, which rang out just as one man let go a shrieking "Whoop!"

Without thinking, Albra instinctively leaned over the canoe. Staring past her reflection, she watched as a trail of vomit spiralled downward beneath the water.

"What d'ya think Vernon?"

"Put another in her to be sure."

"Don't want her getting up again."

A man in greasy overalls stepped out from the group. "Hold her boys."

"What's wrong, Bottom?"

"Bottom's gonna skin her."

"I say give her another one."

The man named Bottom glanced toward the canoe. "Looks like we upset yer girl," he called.

The other men looked up in complete amazement.

Eddie laughed and waved. "She'll be alright!"

Recoiling from their sight, Albra shrunk inside the canoe. Pressing her face into her sleeve, she gagged quietly on the taste.

The boat rocked slightly as Calvin turned it around. "She's fine," he said, as if to himself. His voice remote, matter of fact.

"Last time one o'them eats my dinner . . ."

Bottom nodded solemnly and stepped back into the group of men.

Shooting both animals a final time, the men began to skin the bodies.

Only once on the way back did her father address her.

"There, there," he murmured. "There, there."

The next day the sun was almost up when Albra woke, and from the bedroom window she watched her father's back as they paddled into the grey light. The canoe disappeared beneath the shadow of trees along the shore, only their wake showing as it folded across the water with patient grace. All the time Albra gazed after them, hoping. But he did not look back. Not once.

That evening she waited until her father had gone down to dinner. She found the shirt he had worn hanging behind the door. With a hunted look she pressed the heavy cloth against her face. There, mingled with the acidic taint of tobacco, were memories of the open water, the hills dark in the distance.

Crying to herself, she kissed the cotton sleeves, still damp.

From that day, Albra woke each morning as Eddie and her father lifted the canoe into the water. Through the cold ache of morning, she tormented herself with seizures of brooding. Gazing through the window above her bed, she watched the lone canoe working its way up the lake amid the mist and almost lightless sky. With open eyes she remembered the tusks of ancient trees, lurking pale and ghostly beneath the water. Again, Albra saw her own reflection gliding along the lake's surface, concealing the void below.

☙

Towards their last week at the Highland, Eddie declared that the only decent bait to be found lay under the hotel's verandah. The truth was that the cave-like atmosphere beneath the Inn offered the perfect location to meet with the other boys, free from the censure of mothers and nosy waiters. Here they could smoke and talk freely, arguing over the fish they had caught and the girls they hadn't.

About this time the mood of the hotel was stifled by three days of rain. The resulting cold and dampness forced most guests inside to play cards in the dining room, or to congregate on the great sofas about the fireplace. One of the guests, a member of parliament named Sidney Phelps, entertained the ladies by playing excerpts from *My Lady's Garter*, which he had seen the previous winter in Ottawa.

Below the verandah, Paul and Albra huddled as close as they dared to Eddie and some of the older boys. With the hushed awe of a hostage, Albra stared at the cigarette hanging with contrived insolence from Eddie's mouth. Above them she could hear the deeper voices of several male guests watching the rain. Among these was her father.

For two days, Calvin Creighton had endured the restless energy of children and the extorted politeness of adults. This third day, however, had driven him to drink. He sat now among the other men, nursing both a brandy and a grudge against the rain which battered mockingly atop the boat house.

Having exhausted the women's musical interest, Phelps came to sit with the other men on the verandah. "Damn rain."

Several men nodded assent. Outside, away from families, their conversations were suspended by long intervals of silence. The creak of Phelps' chair snapped this trance.

"Where was all this rain when Parliament was burning?"

Calvin frowned. Over the last few days, the politician's flamboyance had come to grate on him.

"Never mind your bloody Parliament. What about my holiday?"

"Not going out?"

Calvin was relighting his cigar. "Not today, Sidney."

"That girl of yours has taken to fishing."

Calvin surprised himself by frowning again.

A waiter emerged with Phelps' Scotch and soda.

"Of course, Edward's the better angler," Calvin replied. "But . . ." his voice trailing off with confusion, "well, she tries harder to . . . to understand."

"She's her father's daughter," someone muttered by way of closing the topic.

From the corner of the group came a restless creaking of wicker.

"I noticed your other son. The younger one." Phelps had spent seven years as a trial lawyer before entering politics and knew a chink in a man's armour when he saw one.

Calvin stiffened.

"He's often with your wife. He sings wonderfully, you know. Soprano, I think." Phelps gave him a grin, all teeth.

Standing, Calvin ground the cigar under his heel. Below, his children held their breath as the orange embers descended on them.

From where she huddled, Albra could feel Eddie's rage swelling.

One of the other boys choked back a giggle.

Albra held her breath, waiting for her father's reply.

It did not come. Instead, there was only the sharp rasp of his steps moving to the other end of the verandah.

Beside her, Paul was crying softly.

That night Albra woke as her brother got out of bed—the spot where his body had been suddenly filling with cold. Drawing the sheets about her, she lay half-listening for him to return. But after a while his absence began to nag at her, and with great resentment she slipped from the bed's easy warmth.

Finding him nowhere in their room, Albra grew worried and began searching the darkness of the hotel. When this, too, proved fruitless she decided to look outside.

The lake was bathed in cold silence, and her feet grew numb as she walked down to the dock. Watching the stars' reflection on the lake, her eyes caught a round object the size of a dinner plate just under the surface, large and silver like a sunken mirror.

Albra screamed, her voice shattering against the hard sky. And from the lake she felt an invisible appendage drawing her down. Her voice suddenly disappeared beneath the surface and she was left in the liquid darkness. Against her side she felt his open hand pulling at her. Barely visible in the feeble moonlight, his body seemed far away from her; she watched with terror as his thrashing abruptly ceased and his limbs grew still.

Then somewhere above them, an arm smashed through the surface of the lake, and Albra watched the fingers straining to catch them as they began to sink. Inside she felt the strain in her chest, tenuous and desperate. And then, with the impulsive resolution of instinct, she reached out and pushed herself beyond her brother's grasp. As long as she would live, that image would never leave her: his face sinking deeper into the cold heart of the lake, eyes aflame with betrayal.

In an instant Paul had slipped away. Their lives shorn in half.

Perhaps the thing that most haunted Calvin from that night was the sound of his daughter's scream, hearing it over and over in his head until it was released in the last hours of his own life.

When he got down to the dock, he was already feeling the horror of his position, sensing he had failed some primordial test: something a man like Phelps could exploit, a man with no family and no woman except one he could buy for an hour. But all this faded the instant Calvin saw them there together and his chest nearly burst with the hope that it was not too late. Then without thinking, he was reaching in the water, straining to grasp them both and cursing the fact that he could not swim.

When Calvin pulled her from the lake, he was appalled to find Albra limp and silent. As he lifted her into the chilled air, he shook the heavy little body until her head rocked forward and let out a wail that shuddered through her whole being.

"I've got you," he whispered. "I've got you, now."

Held in her father's grasp above the lake, Albra emerged beneath a wake of images which seemed to spill from some severed artery inside her. Shuddering, she saw again the girl under the train, and her own limbs flinched in sympathy for the dismembered figure. Wrenched from that girl's parted mouth was a cry, almost lost in the train's howl, raw and savage like the cornered bear's, whose last glimpse of life was that of men clutching guns for their own protection.

two

For as long as Gabriel could remember, death had hung like a shadow over his life. His father, Thomas Oban, had emigrated from Scotland in search of work, and found it in the Hamilton steel mills. Gabriel had become ill during the voyage to Canada, and nearly died from a fever which had left him weakened. It was only now, in his fifteenth year, that he began showing promise. The family's physician, a Dr. Lafferty on James Street across from the Armoury, suggested the boy sleep outside as a final measure.

"Night air," shrugging his tight, woolen shoulders. "Night air will help him as well as anything." So every evening Gabriel slept outside in the family's backyard. Those principal years of childhood and puberty were spent in the battered chair his father carried out for him. Sitting beneath a canvas awning, the boy nested in a cocoon of sweaters and an old coat of his father's smelling of ore dust and fire.

As a child, his mother pulled him about town on errands in a small wagon, while his older brother Hal ran ahead. Seeing other women on the street she would nod with distanced civility, never pausing to speak. An intensely private woman, Mary Oban lived alone with her pride, trying to hide the fact that everything she loved was broken.

When his health allowed it, Gabriel was sent out to work in the yard where Mary tried to supplement the family diet. It was a simple garden. The soil was mostly hard and uncooperative, and what seeds did persevere were often unhealthy and crooked as plants. Alone in that secluded island of earth, Gabriel worked at pulling weeds or breaking clods of dirt into workable fragments. In the end, life won out against soil and weeds, and most of the family meals were improved by the boy's efforts.

Dinners were an arena for the family to talk and argue, digesting the world around them along with their meal. With each mouthful the children took in their parents' ideas of politics, work, commerce, and, of course, the War.

"I waved to the soldiers," Mona said, using a moment of silence to get a word in.

"Did you then?" Thomas's voice was warm and they could all feel him protecting her.

"Mona is your sister," Mary had said. But she wasn't. Mona was a cousin. And even though she came with them from Scotland, she was not a sister and never would be. Gabe was sure of this from the start.

But she was special, and if anyone ever made Mona cry Thomas would strap the offender.

"You know better," he had warned Gabe and his brother.

When they finished eating, Gabe would wait quietly as his mother cleaned the kitchen. Then, taking the bucket of garbage out back, he emptied it on the heap next to the garden. From the window above him he could hear the family talking together. Here he listened as their words mingled in the soft dusk. Sometimes Mona would find her hymn book, her voice carrying out into the night where he stood:

O how glorious and resplendent,
Fragile body, shalt thou be,
When endued with so much beauty,
Full of health, and strong and free,
Full of vigour, full of pleasure,
That shall last eternally.

In the dark Gabe could trace the sweet odour of his father's tobacco as it mingled in the city's breath. A cricket called from the lawn; beyond the fence, a dog. Odours from the garden rose and embraced him with familiar arms. Kneeling there behind the house, the boy followed the last ray of light as it fell beyond the neighbour's roof, burying his tiny form in darkness.

Night further softened the noises about him, so that the sounds of automobiles and doors, yelling husbands and children, all seemed far away. Then, forgetting the city, he gazed up at the emerging stars with flakes of eggshell digging into his knees. Pins of light began surfacing amid the oil-blue of night, and he studied the birth of each one with sympathy.

These were the kindest moments in Gabriel Oban's youth.

On days she finished her work early, Mary would walk out to the garden where her son was working and rest beside him on the grass. Together in the gilt recline of afternoon, Gabriel and his mother waited for the others to come home.

Mary looked about at the encroaching shadows, stretching across the sooty brick of her home.

"Father's late today," the boy said, reading her thoughts.

"We might do better planting the beets against the wall there," as if she had not heard him. "Mr. Mahonia next door was eating beets in November last year. They stay warm next to the house, he says."

Behind them they heard the loud slap of the side door.

The boy's head looked out from among the leaves.

Sighing, Mary drew herself up. "Better get washed."

"Be in soon."

"Don't you be late now . . ."

Wiping off his hands on a patch of lawn, Gabe could hear his parents talking in the kitchen.

"Where've you been?"

"Am I late for something?"

"I can see what you've been doing."

"And what of it?"

"You know how I feel about it," her voice cold, warning. "Not with the children about."

"Sure, sure. Are we eating then?"

"Where were you?" she demanded.

Thomas sighed benignly. "Just out with the fellows."

Mary rarely met them, these fellows. They were little more than faces she came to recognize. They were ambiguous forms mostly, well-meaning men whose faces bore the restless endurance of their existence.

But among them there was one specifically who Mary looked for. The one named Gopnik. In most respects he appeared no different from the others: he was about middle age and of average height, his thinning, brown hair tucked under a grey slouch hat like the others. He was generally alone when he appeared, his shoulders drawn slightly back as though in a state of restraint. Outwardly, little separated this man from any other; Mary came to know Gopnik not by his appearance, but by the mood in which her husband returned after being out with him.

"You're later than usual."

"What of it?"

"You've an early morning is all."

"All? All I got is my sweat, and they care precious little for that."

"You left here in a good enough mood. You haven't been fighting have you?"

"Oh they'd like that wouldn't they? Keep us fighting among ourselves. Goppy's right—keep us at each other's throats and we'll never see who's really swallowing the cream!"

Gopnik was among the masses of itinerant workers that migrated across Canada in the first quarter of the twentieth century. A class unto themselves, they were a fluid, almost gypsy population that flowed from one industrial centre to another, swelling and depleting urban populations from Halifax to Yellowknife in tides of migration.

Among this group were the bitter disciples of Europe's failed idealism. Here, radicals found a fraternity of anger that allowed them to mingle and preach an ideology of suffering and self-righteousness. In the flop houses and rail cars where they congregated, political tastes ranged from disenchanted socialists to the more rabid followers of Marx. Of the latter, Gopnik was surely one.

He had been involved in the shooting at the city's street car strike in 1906. The real feather in his cap, though, was his sabotage of the offices of Cataract Power, hanging by his knees from the rafters as he wired dynamite into their ceiling. The police had searched half-heartedly in the wreckage, but few thought the saboteur likely to have survived.

Gopnik was an instant hero among those who had instigated the scheme. Seven years later, three spent in the west and the last four mining in the north, Gopnik had returned to Hamilton and the lap of Mother Steel, restless with what he saw as the union's passive tactics to better its members' lives. "Sitting and talking, sitting and talking—that never smashed Cataract! That's just what they want from us. It's bullshit. Wait till they're sitting and kick 'em in the balls. Then they'll listen, and pay up too."

After openly challenging the union there, Gopnik had left more or less on the run, returning to Hamilton where so much former success had been enjoyed. But the men who knew him—and what he had done for them in 1906—had long since left and Gopnik found himself alone. When the War broke out, he landed a good job at one of the mills. Gopnik was well-suited for the work, and he realized this. From his vantage on the floor of Leda Steel, Gopnik could gaze into the ovens' molten froth, finding a sympathy there for the rage that steeled his heart.

෩

Approaching Hamilton harbour, Leda Steel was first identifiable by the musk of burnt ore in the air. Halfway down Victoria Street, the first of the loading cranes became visible above the steady ranks of homes. Stretching beyond the eye, the plant could only be seen in its entirety from the lake. From there, the shore was clogged with mountains of coal and smoke stacks that reached like fingers into the sky.

Earl Pryce looked out the window of his office onto the plant below him. He was not a large person by any measure, though in the two or three photographs that remain of him one senses there were dimensions to this man which transcended the limits of his stature. As is usually the case with photographs, one is drawn first to the man's eyes. His gaze reaches out from the black and white celluloid, leaving one with the feeling of having been analyzed, dissected by the dead.

In his right hand Earl played with a pencil, passing it over and over through his fingers as though winding some internal clock. He had inherited his nervous energy from his mother, after whom he had named the company. Several times each day, he would stop what he was doing to let his imagination wander beneath the enclosures of iron and brick to the furnaces where his steel was conceived. Like the larger institutions along the city's anaemic horizon, there inside the womb of his mill was forged the skin and skeleton of nations.

Leaving his jacket, he descended several flights of stairs to the street where he followed the delivery lane that led to the loading yards. Then, coming to a small flight of stairs, he disappeared into his mill. Inside he had to pause for his eyes to adjust to the dim light. As his vision returned, Pryce saw he was standing among several piles of metal chaff waiting to be thrown back into the oven. Passing beneath a grid of rib-like trestles, he stepped quickly through an enormous corridor furrowed with ingot moulds. Almost two storeys above him hung a crane supporting a ladle for pouring molten steel. Men here tended the ovens. These were unearthly-looking figures, stained as red and black as ants by the cooling steel. Beyond this he stepped out into one of the yards where the steel was stored for shipping. It was an impressive sight, he thought. Each ingot was twice his height, and stood waiting in the yard like some South American shrine. Crossing over the cinders littered about the docking area, Pryce walked toward a large entrance at the other end of the yard. About the doorway the air quivered with heat, and Earl was forced to loosen his collar. Here he was met by an older man who stood with his shirt open in the afternoon sun.

"Hullo."

Pryce stopped. "How're they doing?"

"Bit of indigestion."

"Problem's in the ore."

"Always been a worry. Ovens don't like to be fed something uncertain. Take Number Two there. Irregular as a pregnant bitch that way. Her notch clamps up for no reason and suddenly you have a blow out all round you. And when she's done, don't she go back to purring like nothing happened."

Earl nodded in a matter-of-fact way.

"That's what got the Benton man."

"Bad blow there." The man stopped thoughtfully to scratch the hair on his chest. "Was the ore, too, you know."

"He wasn't paying attention," Pryce said, becoming defensive.

The man they spoke of, Will Benton, had had his arm nearly incinerated the month before by a burst of liquid iron that blew unexpectedly from the converter he was tending. Benton had been his shift's best melter, and the loss of his talent in judging the steel's purity had hurt the plant's output. Pryce felt resentful of Will Benton, and the topic chafed an unacknowledged nerve within him.

One might ask why Pryce should bother to examine the ruder corners of his mill with such interest, why he should ruin the expensive shirts bought by his wife to brave the hazards of the mill floor. Had he been an Ottoman lord, Earl Pryce would have been jealous of the eunuchs who bathed his concubines. Jealous because the thing he loved was groomed by other men, and he suspected she really loved them more than himself. If he were to admit it he would concede his hatred for these men who fed and tended Leda Steel. Such is the way with so many of history's potentates, who, on the eve of what would become their most defining moment, suppress the very sympathies that might have made them great. And all for love—a thing history has never cared a damn about.

When his tour was completed, Pryce drove home through the neighbourhoods where his employees lived. About the gutters and sidewalks lay the stubs of exhausted cigarettes, smoked almost to their tips by men used to drawing the last ounce of marrow from any bone thrown their way. The tenements closest to the plant were awkward structures in various stages of repair. Such homes were mostly used as rental housing. Here the country's new immigrants wandered into beds rented by the week, living this way only until they had saved enough money to move on. Lying among the cramped bedrooms, one heard above the snoring the murmur of a dozen languages: Portuguese and Serb, Yiddish and Pole, all mumbling together in nocturnal council.

In front of his car, a young girl hung out of a trolley loaded with weekenders. Earl waved to get the child's attention, but she was too preoccupied with a billboard being erected beside the road:

> *Just Like a Mother's Milk:*
> *Glaxo*
> *Builds Bonnie Babies*

At the next corner Earl turned off, watching the child until the trolley vanished behind a shop front.

Pryce lived with his wife, Penny, on a small farm outside of the city. At one time, the house had been part of a larger estate that was sold off in pieces when corn prices bottomed out. Earl rented his land to a local man named Jarvis Mekes, who for the past year had worked the soil and grazed several of his cattle on the farm. Mekes could be found tramping about the farm at any time of day, sometimes on a cart or leading a stray cow back to the field.

As he drew up the lane, Earl waved to his wife who sat in a chair on the large open verandah that circled the house. Penny Pryce was slim, though not athletic; and within her frame hung that air of detached poise that men find alluring. Yet behind this enamel of optimism lay an anxious sensitivity to the world, and since her marriage five years earlier she had begun showing the strain of quiet worry.

As her husband approached the house, Penny made an effort to stand.

"Hello, Earl."

Lately she used a sweetened voice when talking with her

husband, unconsciously elongating the first syllable of each word as if trying to draw him closer.

His reply came crisp and alert. "Dear."

"Late at the office?"

He smiled apologetically. "Couldn't be helped."

"I took Mavis back to town this morning. The time we've had! She said to . . . what happened to your shirt?"

Earl looked down at the dust and soot he had collected from his walk through the mill.

"I'll try to be more careful."

"That shirt cost three dollars. I should have gone with the cheaper ones at G. W. Robinson. But I know you like to look good for your men. I'm lucky to have a husband who understands the importance of appearances. Wives have the worst time with their men. Most husbands I know would walk about with two different shoes on for all they cared."

"Dinner at six?"

"Whatever suits you," she smiled. "Fix yourself some lemonade. I left some by the counter."

When he returned, Earl sat in a green wicker chair across from his wife. It was terribly hot and after a little more talking, husband and wife sat together in silence. However, after a few minutes, Penny seemed to grow restless again as though just remembering something.

"Is it true your men are causing problems?"

She now spoke quickly and to the point, betraying a hidden earnestness.

"Where did you hear that?"

Penny brushed at an invisible fly. "Mavis said . . . she asked if that's why we lived in the country," squinting to search her husband's eyes. "I told her, of course not, that you preferred it here because of your childhood."

There was a brief pause while Earl stared into his empty glass.

"I wouldn't have mentioned it except that the thought of those . . . well, I was worried."

"Whatever for?"

Penny laid her book across her knees, her voice dropping. "It's nothing, surely. Only that there is a resentment I've noticed since the War began. A dislike for those who manage things now. Mostly it's for the government, of course, but men like you as well."

"You've just noticed this now?"

"Recently," she corrected, feeling conscious of something shameful. Like blood on a bathroom tile.

He leaned over her with a paternal air. "There have always been men that challenged me. Look at us; not you and I, but the lot of us. Drive through town and you'll see. We're a disowned race and everyone's looking for a crusade. Nowadays personal ownership is the fastest way to become a heretic."

He bent down to kiss her, his voice softening.

"Do you know what a condemned man longs for, more than anything else?"

"Reprieve?"

He shook his head. "Another condemned man."

Penny looked at him for a long time before she smiled.

He touched the edge of her sleeve hesitantly. "Maybe we could put off dinner . . .?"

Penny lowered her head. "What would be the point?" she whispered.

Earl felt her withdraw. "You're not worrying about that are you?"

"But what are we doing wrong? My sister has . . ."

Earl let his hand drop.

"It will be fine," he said, picking up his glass. "Now can we talk of something else?"

"Alright," her voice retreating. And for several minutes they were silent, looking for something to say. Finally Penny looked up with a strained smile. "Have you heard about that man they tried to kill?"

Earl began to relax. "No, I haven't seen the paper yet."

"But you've heard of J. P. Morgan?"

"Of course."

"It was him. He was shot today."

Earl looked down at the pieces of broken glass about his feet, glittering like diamonds in the afternoon sun.

"My God," he said. "Poor bastard."

℘

Francis Mahonia watched the boy from across the wire fence. "What are you doing there?"

Afraid of getting scalded, Gabe did not look up as he poured out the water.

"I said, what are you doing there?"

When it was empty, Gabe set the pot down. "Killing ants," he replied.

Mahonia frowned.

Gabe looked at the man, pointing at his feet for proof. "See, they're dying."

The ants on the ground lay in little clusters.

"There. All dead."

Mahonia looked at the boy, shaking his head. "They're not all dead."

Gabe gave the anthill another look. "I don't see any left."

"Deep down they're there, waiting for us to leave."

"The water was boiling."

"But what about the ones too far down for the water? That's where the queen lives. If you don't kill her, it don't matter how many you get."

"Why should she matter?"

"If she lives, she keeps having babies.

Gabe looked dubiously at the ant hill. "I still think you're wrong."

"I'm not."

He considered this for a while. "Who's this queen then?"

"She runs the show down there. All the ants you see in your house are women ants, working to feed her and her baby ants."

"There are women ants?"

"Oh yes."

"Where are the men ants?"

"They only exist down below, helping the queen make baby ants."

"She's awfully important."

"The male ants work to mate her until they die, and then one of the young ones replaces the dead one." Mahonia looked hard at Gabe.

Gabe bent down to assess his success. "I guess," he muttered, still unconvinced.

Mahonia tapped him on the shoulder. "Come with me," he said.

Following the man around the back of his house, Gabe waited as Mahonia disappeared into a little shed built against the back fence. Emerging with an armful of tiny jars, the man set them down on the grass.

"Now," he announced. "I will show you how to kill ants."

The boy looked doubtfully at the collection of jars. "What's all that?"

"Quiet. You watch." Kneeling on the grass, Mahonia took a long-handled spoon and began dipping into each jar, placing varying portions of powder into a small bowl. When he was done, the man motioned the boy to lean closer.

"Now, spit in here," he said holding out the bowl. "Careful now, not on my hand."

When the boy had deposited enough spittle into the bowl,

Mahonia began stirring it and the powder together until it had balled itself into a brown paste. "Here." He handed the boy his bowl. "Take this."

As the man predicted, the ants had reappeared atop their home in panicked droves. Mahonia directed the boy as he dabbed small portions about the hill. "Don't touch it with your hands."

"What would happen?"

"It's poison."

Gabe's eyes grew wide. "Poison?"

"You won't get them by drowning."

"What will it do?"

"Watch as they carry it away. They're taking it to their queen. But when she eats it . . ."

Looking back, Gabe would remember it as a pristine summer, full of sunshine and hours in his garden. In many ways, this was the last summer of his childhood, where mornings still lasted all day. At night, too, there was new life. In the drowsy humidity, he listened to the neighbour's Victrola and the whine of mosquitoes.

The black arm bands, once only heard of over dinner tables, now began appearing on streets and trolleys. He was awed that people would do something that made others look, announcing suffering with such openness. Gabe had also noticed the oak pews of women at church, their faces set in powdered masks of grief and hope as the new lists were read. Necks bent with humble forbearance, accepting the War as they would the birth of a deformed child or the existence of God.

Gabe sensed there was something grand and serious taking place. Yet like a passenger in a speeding train, he still saw the War as a machine—apart from himself, unaware that his life had become part of the momentum. Through all this motion, life adapted itself to the country's new grief; in a little while Gabe stopped the exhaustive recognition of individual suffering. He left that up to God, Who counted the sparrows.

Mary and Gabe often shopped in the city market. As they walked, Gabe listened to the vigour in the city's voices, staring wide-eyed at the posters and graffiti tacked to walls and fences. Out of shops came women fortified behind careful dresses of crêpe de Chine, stopping here and there to talk with acquaintances. Here, too, were alien smells, the orphaned appetites of Europe crated and plucked in malodorous stalls.

From these clusters of hips and arms rang out the deafening sincerity of commerce.

As the summer drew on, Gabe's brother, Hal, became increasingly tense. He was in trouble more often now, as though he feared the opportunity might not last forever, his energy venting itself in reckless indulgences. Thomas merely gave the boy extra distance, while Mary remained resolute in the face of this hormonal storm. But Hal refused to surrender his personality to her, the way his brother had. And so he lashed out at her, finding in his rage a self-expression previously unknown to him.

"You don't even love me!" the boy would accuse.

Mary looked up from the bird she was plucking. "You've no idea."

"Oh really?" It was the best he could do by way of rebuttal.

"That's right," she snapped. "Now use some of your energy and help your brother with the table."

"I won't!" he insisted, seeing an opportunity for dissent. "I'm going outside!"

"It's about time," she said when he had gone.

And so Mary went on firmly loving Hal and his resistant heart the same as she loved Gabe with his weak one. For Mona, she felt a fondness and duty, but for the boys there was fierce and unremitting love. Few dreams existed for Mary Oban, only the instinct to protect what was hers, that love forced upon the oddly incapable hands of the parent. There was no meaning in meals or clean floors or labour, only the formula of physical maintenance. But through Hal and Gabe, her yearning for purpose was satiated.

Beneath Mary's austerity was a bond to each child that she was unable to resist. Thrust upon her, she had struggled at first with the agony of this unwanted union to other beings. But it was in the feebleness of her youngest son that she realized the extent of her entrapment. Life insisted on suffering, for pain brought purpose.

Each spring Mary and Thomas Oban took Mona and their two sons to the highest point on York Boulevard, overlooking Hamilton harbour. After several years these outings seemed to Gabe an extension of the season, with their own rituals and sublimated forms of significance. Once they had eaten the meal Mary had packed, the boys went off on their own to explore along the path. Scavenging there among the crusts and refuse of the ignorant, they sought out pennies and other lost treasures so pivotal to a child's belief in destiny.

It was not until much later, when his mother continued to go to that spot alone, that Gabe understood what they were doing and why. In the minds of Mary and Thomas persisted the belief that beyond the water, no matter how far, was Maybole, that home of all things lost.

Even Gabe, the youngest in the family, remembered a little of the Ayrshire town. They were fragments mostly, edges of a mental photo long since lost. Stoking the stove at home Gabe found the place in the coal smoke, an odour woven into the distant fabric of that life. It carried faces and sounds that he could not account for. There were the old men who let him hold their pipes, the boozy gait of fellows about Carrick's, and the rain-blackened ribs of Crossraguel.

And then suddenly the quiet rhythm of the town was

swept aside, blown like confetti over the railing of the ship that carried his family into the wind. In his mind, he was alone on the deck with Hal and the girl and his mother's angry sobbing. Looking about, Gabe knew the world had changed, that something solid beneath his feet had been replaced with a more fluid destiny. Because of this he stayed close to Mary, clung to the edge of her dress for all its blunt comfort. For days, Gabe watched the water stretch into the horizon. In this way, he began to forget what the old men had said, and he felt alone for all the water between him and their stories.

The food his mother brought had to last clear across the Atlantic, or as close as they could manage. He watched her raise a piece of bread to her lips as if to eat it, and then slip it back into the trunk where the food was kept. The boy saw how she worried and so he ate what she gave him, even when it had gone bad. And at night he fought back tears as the pain started in his belly, the whole time wondering what was happening to the world.

But this too had passed, and one day they were met at a train station by a man who picked Gabe up and tossed him in the air.

Mother said this was his father.

"Doesn't he recognize me?"

"He was so young when you left."

"Two years ain't all that long. You remember your dad, don't you boy?"

Gabe had drawn the hard material of her dress between him and this man. Then the boy watched the way he embraced her. He had never seen a man touch his mother.

But these thoughts were soon lost in a flurry of elbows and voices through which they were led to that orange brick house. His mother was pleased, Gabe could tell, when she saw the tiny house and Thomas told her it was all theirs and they didn't have to share it like the one in Scotland.

"Even a plot out back in case you're inclined to plant a little something," he said, and this had made her smile.

This happened just before Gabe took sick, before the fever that almost killed him.

ഇ

In the summer of 1916, Mary Oban was called to the home of her neighbour, Beatrice Mead. For two days, Mary waited and held the woman's pale hand. But when the child's head finally appeared, it was macerated and blackened with almost a week of rot at the bottom of its mother's womb. Almost dead herself, Beatrice tried rising to see the child.

"Is it beautiful?" Beatrice gasped, delirious.

"Lie back," Mary said.

The woman's lips were scabbed and bloody where she'd bitten through during the worst of it. "I can almost see it," Beatrice whispered.

Unwilling to disturb the woman's body further, Charles Mead asked that they bury the half-seen child as it was. "It'll do no good now," he said, looking down on the split and dissipated body of his wife.

When the undertaker and his assistant arrived, along with the doctor, Mary arranged the woman's hands. Sitting in a chair by the corner, she watched as the two men began measuring.

"You write those figures down. I don't want to fold this one."

"Over there in the book."

"Right."

The assistant paused over the woman. "What about this?" he said, pointing.

"God, I don't know . . . can't push it back in can you?"

"You're kidding me."

"Yeah," he said, glancing at Mary. "We'll worry about that later. Just get the legs straightened or you'll only have to measure again when she's cleaned up."

"Right. Pass me the stick, will you?"

She sat a long time looking upon the woman's body. A bleached pallor overcame Mary, and gradually a line drew across her jaw. Sitting there, she recalled something a teacher had once made her recite:

> *Oh, still I behold thee,*
> *All lovely in death,*
> *Reclined on the lap of thy mother,*
> *When the tear trickled bright,*
> *When the short stifled breath,*
> *Told how dear ye were aye to each other.*

As a girl, Mary remembered the verse sounding so beautiful.

The undertaker's assistant became uncomfortable and lit a cigarette, trying to ignore her. Mary watched a piece of ash settle on the woman's mouth as he leaned over.

The doctor and undertaker were consulting by the bed.

"Shall I take that out? I have a clamp in the car for the purpose."

"Doesn't make much sense."

"It's a messy business at any rate. Besides, it'll be cheaper in a single casket."

In the kitchen, Mary passed Charles Mead who was being comforted by his eldest daughter. He leaned on the table, both hands supporting his head.

"What will I do?" he moaned.

Mary returned home and slept for most of the day; when she rose that evening, she found Thomas watching her from a stool at the window. Seeing her stir, he stood slowly, tucking a hand under each arm.

"You alright?"

Mary pushed back the hair from her eyes.

"Saw them take her out," he replied. In the shadows, his wife's face was hidden from him.

Mary nodded, her head slow and heavy with sleep.

Thomas shifted quietly.

"Are you hungry?"

"No."

Thomas sighed, unsure of what to say next. There was a pause, and when he spoke again his words were quiet. "From the way you look, you probably ain't slept for awhile."

"How could I?" her voice aching with restraint.

"It is a hard thing," making an effort to agree with her.

Mary was almost standing now, leaning against the bed for support. "It was like watching an execution," she whispered. "And what did her husband say when she lost the child? That she wasn't strong enough. As if they wouldn't shoot any man on the Front to put him out of that much pain. But that's different isn't it? A man's pain is always about death."

Thomas stepped forward, confused by the hostility in her tone. "You can't go blaming Charlie. He's probably beside himself right now."

"His suffering is meaningless. When it's all said and done he can only look on. When a woman gives birth there is only her, the child, and the pain. That is the trinity of life."

Mary frowned when he did not reply, watching him back against the wall. "I can't be part of it any more Thomas. You should know this. I won't be taken out of this house in a casket's belly with a dead child still lying in my own. We've got the two boys at least. And Mona. I'm sorry Thom. I won't— you can't have that anymore. Not with me."

Thomas stood in the widening silence, his wife's shadow fading completely as night settled upon them.

The easy-going manner that had made his marriage to Mary viable now betrayed Thomas. Unable to contest her decision, he was left reeling with confusion and bitterness.

The next morning, Thomas moved into the room that had been Gabe's before he was sick. From that day on Thomas slept alone, his feet sticking off the end of the bed. In the morning, he rose to find Mary making his breakfast as usual. Eating in silence, he occasionally glanced at his wife, her own gaze fixed rigidly on the task in front of her. Had he been a keener man, Thomas might have recognized the struggle in his wife's face, but as it was, he saw only her mute determination to avoid him. With a sense of being forsaken, he turned back to his meal. When he was done, he stood up and brushed the crumbs from his shirt, grabbing his lunch at the door.

"Bye," he offered. But there was only silence behind him as he stepped out into the dark street.

Thomas Oban stood patiently with the three men who worked under him. On the second whistle, he looked up instinctively as the drums of ore loomed towards him, drawn across the ceiling on huge conveyors. The oven seemed to swell with heat as the ore thawed to a red placenta. Thomas watched it carefully, mentally calculating the altering shades of molten iron as it incubated. Motioning to the ladler, he knelt at the oven's groin, helping to steady the man's grip. Retreating together from the open furnace, the man poured the metal into a small mould. When it had partially cooled, another man picked the steel out of its mould with a pair of tongs while Thomas broke off the end with a hammer. The crew leaned forward as he checked the grain. Half an hour passed and the process was repeated.

A man came by pulling a large barrel on a cart. Two at a time the men from each crew gathered to pour water over their heads until the soot and grime collected about their necks in black creases.

Gopnik waited at the barrel until Thomas approached, handing him a tin for scooping the water. "You'll want this."

Thomas knocked it away. Then he dunked himself up to the shoulders. Lifting himself out, he spewed a mouthful of water in their direction and gave himself a slap on the chest.

"Cold as my wife's arse in January!" he howled.

Gopnik punched him in the chest.

Thomas grinned with distraction.

If the weather was fine, Thomas liked to eat his lunch in a corner of the loading yard where he could watch the steel being loaded onto ships. He enjoyed wondering what would become of it, following each ingot as the crane lifted it from the dock like a cat with her kittens. Here he was able to take in the workings of the plant and all its doings: the moan of gears and straining equipment, the yells of workers above the maelstrom of the ovens, and at the end of it all a posterity whose every feature testified to its origin—man made.

When the day ended, Thomas and Gopnik often went looking about the city for diversions. Ambling into Gomph's Brewery, they tried swatting the behind of Annie Booth and other picketers from her Temperance League. They clucked their tongues and winked at any woman who challenged them. The two men sat in the mismatched chairs against the wall, Gopnik rocking back so as to push his cap over his eyes. They sat like this for sometime, talking aimlessly as they drank.

Later Gomph came up to take their glasses. "Six o'clock Thom; you not going home?"

Thomas caught the man's wrist in a friendly way but the grip dug hard. "Why don't you mind your own business?"

Glancing at his friend, Gopnik reached into his shirt pocket and handed Gomph a coin.

"We'll have two more when you've a moment . . ."

Afterward, the two men walked for a while, looking into shops with penniless curiosity.

"Did you see those union types in there? Doing what they do best, whining about the rights of the forsaken worker. Blah, blah," Gopnik spat onto a passing street car. "A man shouldn't negotiate for what is his. He should take it, no asking about it. Thomas? You listening?"

"Yeah . . ."

Gopnik looked at him closely, evaluating. "You agree, don't you?"

"What would I be agreeing with?"

"If another man had taken your wife from you, you wouldn't ask for her back would you? No! You'd take her back."

Thomas looked down, his face grim and set in shadow. "Aye. I'd take her. But I'd kill the bastard first."

Gopnik's eyes lightened.

"That's right! That's exactly right. See," patting Thomas on the chest. "We think alike, you and I. Those fools back there, thinking a union will represent them! How can men like us stomach them? I want to puke with all the shit they shove down our throats about representation. Uniting the worker! Bullshit. Let me tell you something, friend; I almost resent the union more than I do Pryce and his lot. They stand between me and my right to take what is mine . . . ours. Those of us who work for a living and get half a one in return. Like it isn't us who make the steel in the first place . . ."

Thomas stared ahead, mulling over Gopnik's words which fell like coal on the smouldering flame inside him.

Such was the world to which Thomas Oban fled, seeking a diversion among Gopnik's rhetoric, a bandage for the void that hung between him and his wife. If Thomas spent more time now with Gopnik, it was because he had little else to do with himself besides go home, and there he found only anger and confusion. Interspersed, however, between these moments of fraternal diversion were hours, eroding often into days, of extreme loneliness during which the full vacuity of his life seemed to crush upon him. The numbing ache of it soon left him dangerously vulnerable to distraction.

Late into one shift Thomas had drawn near the oven to check on a new load of ore. But instead of pulling back he paused, momentarily mesmerized by the fire. Crusts of iron broke against the oven's sides, only to be pushed inward where they vanished in a yolk of molten steel. Thomas's legs began to shake, resisting. A flash of blue erupted as a cavity of gas was purged.

Then suddenly a hand drew him back from the oven, and Thomas choked down a sob as water was thrown over him.

"What the hell were you thinking? Your own hair caught fire!"

He looked up helplessly at Gopnik. There were other men standing over him now, and Thomas used his sleeve to hide his face.

"Damn water's in my eyes."

Gopnik glanced at the other men. "Back to it. He's alright."

He reached down to offer Thomas his hand. "Can you get up?"

"Course I can."

As Thomas stood he drew close to Gopnik, his voice dropping to almost a whisper. "Goppy . . ."

"Shut up," he interrupted. "It was nothing. Just the fire playing tricks."

"Yeah."

Gopnik looked hard at Thomas, their faces medieval and furtive in the oven's glow. "You'd have done the same for me, wouldn't you?"

"Course I would."

"Good." He let go of Thomas's arm. "I watch out for my own."

Water ran about the scorched crust of his beard, dancing in the oven's glow until each rivulet seemed as liquid fire.

"I owe you, Goppy," he said, trying to smile.

"Owe me? Shit."

The two men looked at each other.

"Alright then," Thomas drew his hand across his face. "Back to it."

Gopnik watched as Thomas limped back to his crew.

Around them the ground shook as a bin of ore ground across the trellis above; men scurried into place as it approached. Gopnik watched as his own oven received the load, a splash of liquid fire lapping about its mouth that gaped unsatisfied, craving something more.

かり

"You keep at that and I'll go for more."

"Alright." Gabe sunk his arms deep into the barrel of suds, emerging with a pair of his father's trousers. Gabe normally tired easily, but today he felt invigorated with the odours of soap and wet wool. The autumn sun warmed his back and shoulders.

"Watch out then." Mary nudged the boy aside with her hip before dumping a kettle of boiling water into the barrel.

She glanced sideways at the boy. "You seem better lately."

"Do I?"

Gabe dipped his hands back into the barrel.

"Must be all that time outdoors."

"I like sleeping back here."

Mary shook out the shirt she was scrubbing. "I was referring to your talks with the neighbour there," nodding toward Mahonia's fence. "Goodness knows what the two of you have in common."

"He knows a lot."

"Still, you shouldn't be neglecting our garden."

"He's teaching me how to tend it properly."

"You tell him I'll be very obliged if he can get cabbage to grow in this soil."

The sun rose a little higher as they worked, and Gabe watched the light play against the water.

"Mahonia says there's nothing so mysterious as watching a seed become a plant. It's a transformation, he says."

"Does he?"

"And he says no one really knows why or how it happens, and that secretly we're all afraid because of it."

Mary snorted. "If there's anything that scares a man, it's an immaculate conception."

The two worked for some time before he spoke again.

"Why isn't Hal going to fight?"

"I didn't raise a fine fellow like him just to throw him to the Kaiser."

"That's why he was so mad?"

"He's a hard-headed one."

"But his friends have left."

"And two of them dead already, their mothers ruing the day they had sons."

"Maybe Dad could go and take care of him."

"And what would we do?"

Gabe squinted into the sun to see her face, serious. "I can feed us from the garden."

"No, that won't work."

"Dad would have to get better before they would take him, of course."

Mary stopped working. "What's wrong with your father?"

"Isn't he sick?"

"He's a horse."

Gabe was quiet for a moment. "He's in my old room. I thought maybe he was sick, too."

His mother looked at him, her lips pursing in thought. "It's me that doesn't want to get sick."

"Sick from Dad?"

"Just sick."

Gabe worked on in silence, his eyes widening as a thought dawned on him. His tongue became clumsy and heavy in his mouth.

"Not from me?"

"No."

The boy took a breath. "Good."

"Hungry?"

"Sure am," he said, almost giddy with relief.

∽

Pryce sat in his McLaughlin, waiting for a train to pass. Every now and then a man could be seen jumping away from the tracks. Standing, they brushed the dust from their arms before picking up coats and hats that had fallen among the grass.

There was a tap on his shoulder.

"Hey, mister?" He was a tall, thin man. Dust darkened the creases of his face like the contours on a wilting map.

"Yeah?"

"This Brantford?"

"Not even close."

"Sheeit." The man shook his head, his stare deepening with resignation.

"Brantford's that way," Earl said, pointing southwest down the track.

The man waved at him. "Alright."

When Pryce arrived at his office that morning, two men in grey suits were waiting for him.

"From the Ministry," his secretary whispered.

Earl spent the better part of the morning with these men. At noon he was in a particularly good mood, and when he came back from lunch he spent an hour or two leisurely going through some paperwork. Stuck between the day's mail he found an envelope addressed to him, containing a single piece of paper with the words

what is yours will be ours
our time is coming

written in crude letters.

He held the paper only a moment before tossing it aside. "Rhetoric," he scoffed.

Earl had received this sort of thing before. He had even collected them at one time. Such hate, Pryce knew, was dispensed with no little amount of envy.

But an hour later he walked down to the mill floor looking agitated. From across the floor, Earl watched a sombre young man pacing about one of the crews. Pryce waved at him.

Ernest Gall ascended the stairs to the landing where Earl stood. "Mr. Pryce?"

Earl decided to get right to the point. "What do you think of the workers?"

"How do you mean?"

"Are you happy with them?"

"If you mean are we friends, I'd have to say no. Our relationship is antagonistic by nature."

"By design," Pryce corrected.

"Yes sir. And so there's little opportunity for me to create any feeling toward them."

"Tell me what you think of them?"

Gall glanced over his shoulder. "Too political. For my taste, least-ways."

Earl frowned. "Political?"

"Unions did it to them," gesturing toward the crews below. "Most are very committed unionists, I'd say."

"Yes, yes. I know all about that."

"A few Fabians here and there, among the brighter sort largely."

Pryce nodded.

"Also, one or two radicals."

"What do you mean?"

"Well, you have to expect it, Mr. Pryce. Anywhere you get a group of men, you're bound to have some malcontents. Troublemakers."

"What kind of trouble?"

"Well, like I said, political tensions. You don't need to worry about the union people mostly. You can see them coming a mile away. But . . ."

"But?"

"I see things, you know. Leaflets . . . subversive writing against the War. Among the foreigners, mostly. The Croats and Macedonians. Irish too. Plenty of slogans around."

"Son," Earl purred with abrasive confidence, "I have a problem here you might be able to help me with."

Gall blinked.

"You see things down here that I can't keep on top of on my own. Like this political annoyance you mentioned. You understand why I need to know, don't you?"

Gall nodded.

"There is more going on here than profit. Leda Steel, everything you see here, is mine. Most of the men upstairs wouldn't care if their mothers were down here so long as they had their margins. I'm not like that, you understand? I need to know."

"About the men, sir?"

"Precisely."

"About their goings on?"

"When they affect the workings of my plant, yes. I don't mind telling you that I just took on several contracts connected to the War effort. Considerable contracts . . ." Earl took a moment to let this achieve its effect. "But if there's something uncertain about the men I employ, I want to know about it. I can't afford trouble in my plant, can I?"

Gall was silent, Pryce's breath hot against his ear.

෩

Thomas waited outside the loading area of the mill with two other men.

Gopnik was late. Like Thomas, he worked as a melter running the crew at one of the ovens. On the way off his shift, Thomas had seen Gopnik arguing with Ernest Gall, the chemist recently hired to oversee the quality of the plant's output. He was generally considered an annoyance by the men on the floor.

"What the hell does college boy there know about steel?" Thomas muttered.

The other men shook their heads.

It was a long while before Gopnik finally appeared.

"Sorry, lads. Had some trouble with Pryce's cocksucker. He wouldn't know the grade he wanted if it were coming out his ass. Telling me my job when he can't even do his own . . ." From there Gopnik simmered into a string of profanity.

Thomas looked at him impatiently. "Let's get going."

The four men left the mill, passing out into the bright sunlight of the street. Turning right they joined a crowd of men on their way home. A boy stood in front of the mill, selling papers to the workers as he called out the day's headlines above their heads.

Thomas lighted a cigarette, exhaling a trail of blue smoke into the street. Within a few blocks, they came to a railway track littered with cast-off bits of wood and brick. Following this trail for a mile or two they left the shadow of factories and loading yards for the open fields at the edge of the city.

Stepping off the track where it bridged a steep gully, Gopnik paused to look over his shoulder before following the others down a path running beneath the railway. Hidden in the brush beside the bridge was a stack of ties leaning vertically against the base of the stone wall. Each man ducked beneath the ties, disappearing into a break in the masonry.

Inside they waited as Gopnik lighted a candle. The air was damp and cool. The candle illuminated a surprisingly large chamber almost high enough for the men to stand. Moving forward from the shadows into the light, Gopnik handed a bottle to Thomas.

"Here you are boys. Let the Prohibits be damned!"

Someone lighted a cigarette while the four passed around the bottle, their conversation relaxing slowly as they drank. Gopnik was unusually quiet in his corner, nor did he seem to drink much, but instead studied the faces of the other men. They spoke in a reserved way at first before settling into talk of work.

Sensing the conversation's turn, Gopnik addressed the man beside him. "Joe, I meant to ask after your son. Have you heard anything more?"

Joseph Moylan was a hulking Irishman with four sons, three of them in the War, two of whom had died in the first months of the fighting. The third had disappeared during a frontal assault at Arras. Joe worked as a shoveller on Thomas's crew, a job that put him so close to the oven's heat he rarely had eye brows.

At Gopnik's reference to his son, the man instinctually looked down at his boots. "No word, yet."

Gopnik shook his head.

The other two men looked sympathetically at Joe's shoes. "Sometimes no news is good news," muttered Thomas.

"Yes, sometimes if you're lucky . . ." the other man trailed off in agreement.

Joe stirred irritably. "Do I look lucky?"

Gopnik prodded the large man with the bottle. "Easy, Joseph. You're among friends." Gopnik turned sympathetically to the man who had spoken. "You know, John here would never say anything against you. You know he has troubles like the rest of us, don't you John?"

John Humphrey was a thin man with black unruly hair. He stared back at Gopnik numbly. "Course I do."

"Of course you do," Gopnik echoed. "You can't blame John here for feeling warmly about your troubles, can you? Not when you know what he's been through with his father."

Humphrey looked at Joe. "I know what you're feeling Joe. I do. God knows the foreman gives as much credit to my dad's death as the military gave to your sons'."

"That's a truth," Joe said. "That's a truth."

"Those bastards. I'd like to even things," Gopnik whispered.

They were silent a moment, each smelling the bitterness in Gopnik's breath. The bottle was handed to Thomas, who tilted it upward for a long swallow.

Gopnik turned to him, sensing the moment. "Thom, I see the tear in your eye too. You can't deny it among us, and you don't need to neither. I can see we understand each other. That's clear to me. Just cause you ain't had a death don't mean you ain't hurting from a loss."

Thomas looked at Gopnik blankly, suddenly wanting to swing at him. "How'd you . . ."

Gopnik placed a hand on his shoulder. "Thomas, when you work among friends . . ." he looked to the two other men. "We share a common sympathy for each man and those he loves. Don't bother how we know; only know that we stand by you quietly."

"That's right," John said. "When I heard I only shook my head for you, wishing there was something I might do."

"That's a truth," Joe said. "That's what it is."

Thomas stared at them, still stunned by this confession.

"And your son," Gopnik continued. "The youngest one. Don't think your sufferings over him have gone unnoticed among your fellow workers. Those that stand by you every day, looking into Hell's mouth with you. It's a common bond we share in the ovens, ain't it?" Gopnik looked at them over the candle's glow.

A long silence ensued as each man sat with this thought.

Gopnik pushed aside the bottle as it was handed to him. "No thank you, friend."

The other men stared at him. Even in the candle's half-light, Gopnik could see the watery glaze on each man's eyes, and he grinned suddenly in spite of himself.

"I have something to say."

They heard the wail of a train whistle and almost immediately the tiny chamber began to shudder. Gopnik paused, waiting as the train approached. Like a peal of distant thunder, the rumbling quickly closed on them. Faint trails of dust passed into the candlelight. Then, almost as quickly as it came, the train vanished.

Gopnik couldn't help grinning to himself as he looked around. The three men were now completely, if momentarily, sober.

"I've been listening to your woes for a long time now. And, on occasion, I have been thankful to share my own troubles with you. That's what we're here for, isn't it? That's something the worker can find among his fellows that no owner ever knew."

Joseph nodded solemnly at this. "That's a truth," he murmured.

"And surely I feel for your sufferings, as I know you do for mine. But lately I've seen that we are not the worst off. When I see poor Benton at the hospital with his one arm!"

The three men sat remembering their crippled friend.

"I tell myself every day there are men with more to complain about than us. Aren't there? Shouldn't we be grateful for what we have? Surely we should go home to our families and be thankful that we are not in the shoes of William Benton. Of course, the accident was his fault somehow, wasn't it? Never mind how long that man had worked on the line; never mind that he trained most of us! Surely it was his fault; what could he know?" Gopnik paused again, using his sleeve to wipe the sweat from his face. "That's surely what they want, isn't it? Because when I think about it, when I think about poor Benton I am reminded of our common plight as working men. I see in that broken friend an image of ourselves not in the future, but now, here before us. Isn't this so? Look about; look at yourselves. Have not each of you losses equal to that of Benton's arm? Would not Joe here, for instance, give two limbs for just one of his boys?"

They turned to look at Joe who nodded passionately in reply, his voice too choked for words.

"That's a truth," John whispered for him.

"Sure it is," Thomas echoed.

Gopnik gazed down at them, almost sneering. "Don't weep for Benton, nor even Joe here. You should weep for yourselves. Through our passive consent to these conditions we are all as crippled as poor, one-armed Benton. We are all condemning our sons to destruction. Look at the capitalists! Look how their greed consumes our bodies and our children. Do you think this war is about freedom? How could it be when our own people face a more vicious form of servitude right here?"

Thomas stared back at Gopnik. "You're sounding like a pacifist," he muttered.

"Make no mistake," he hissed. "I'm for war. But war on my terms, against my enemies—against the enemy of the People.

What have we against the Germans compared to Pryce and his lot?"

The other men looked about them, considering his words. The alcohol had taken effect.

Gopnik turned on them now, his voice venomous with disdain. "That's right, look around for an answer. Sitting there drunk as mules—just the way they want you. You're all eunuchs, passing over your labour to the unsoiled hands of your boss. Well, I say that should end. They can't have it both ways! What will you have in twenty years, eh? Shit. But the owners, they'll have an empire to sit on, to hand to their sons. Why do you think Joe's boys died over there, eh? So guys like Pryce could make their fortune. Never forget fellas: wars make steel companies." He paused a moment to let this sink below the alcohol. "So go ahead, Thom. You can go fight the rich man's war. Or you can fight your own."

Thomas was taken back by Gopnik's challenge. "Hey—"

"Hey nothin'. What's it gonna be?" Gopnik held himself back from saying more. He had worked himself up pretty well and his zeal had almost taken him past the turn he had been planning. Gopnik had been planning this moment for weeks, and his chest now ached with pent up energy. Though he wasn't aware of it, he had chosen Thomas for this final thrust that day in Gomph's Brewery.

Thomas stared stupidly at his friend. "Why you picking on me?"

"I ain't pickin' on no one. You haven't answered my question. You with us or against us? You gonna go on fighting your master's battles, or your own?"

Thomas's brow flattened. "I'll be fighting my own. Always have."

Gopnik looked at the other men, who only nodded their support. "No," he said. "You've never fought your own battles. Not till now."

three

Albra could hear them downstairs, moving furniture about for the photograph her father had planned. All that morning she had sat painting in her room, stopping only to go to the station with the others to meet Eddie.

It had been such a shock to see Eddie that way. But now, back in her room she could cry openly for him and paint away her grief. It was here, in the quiet, that Albra could close her eyes and see again the hills in that far-off place. What her memory had received with one stroke would take her brush a thousand to recover.

She had been painting for nearly two years now. Her father had given her the paints and a few frames of canvas after Paul's death, and she had gorged herself on this crumb of affection. She could not help it. Even after his rejection at the Inn, Albra could not help embracing this remote act of pity.

"If you do well at it I will look into getting you lessons," he had promised.

She had almost wept with appreciation. Paul's death had left her bleeding, like a wound that would not heal. That unseen place, where the line between their lives had blurred now lay ripped open, and her father's affection, though awkward and insufficient, seemed to fill this cavity. But for all this, Albra's life now revolved within a sphere of emptiness. It defined her now, more than her brother's life ever had.

Eddie had departed for France shortly after Paul's funeral, overcome, it seemed, with a need to escape from his family. Until he left, Hannah had been absorbed in the numbing succession of duties placed on her. But once Eddied had gone, she slid into a crevice of depression, and it was not until the following June that Hannah began showing signs of recovery.

One morning that summer, Albra had looked out between the curtains of her bedroom window. Below her mother was drinking iced tea in a tumbler of blue glass, listening as Elizabeth read Eddie's letter.

Looking up through the branches, Hannah spied Albra at the window. She waved weakly, but the girl did not see her. Poor child, she thought, and just then Hannah felt a sudden rush of warmth for the girl, thinking she might go upstairs that instant and take Albra in her arms. But the moment passed, and feeling a sudden chill she subsided back into her chair.

Elizabeth stopped reading from the letter. "You're missing him aren't you?"

Hannah nodded, wiping her eyes. "He's been gone so long."

"But he'll be home soon. You'll see."

She was quiet, staring at her fingers.

"Edward. Yes, of course."

Hannah had always been an uncomfortable mother. In her children, she found not an extension of herself but an agonized reflection. Like a shadow, her oldest son had never been hers, passing elusively through her fingers and into his father's hands. With Elizabeth and Laura there was, of course, a stronger bond, but they were more like her apprentices. Only in the twins had she found the enigmatic symmetry of perfection. Now this, too, had been broken.

Though Hannah did not often explore the tributaries of her grief, she was nonetheless aware of a deepening sense of her daughter's betrayal. With confused tears, she remembered the disdain that Albra had shown her, and most of all the girl's open preference for her father's company. At the time, her daughter's slights had seemed a minor annoyance. But viewed now from the depth of her loss, the blame Hannah so badly needed to assign came to rest on her daughter. Had the girl not been so quick to take her brother's place, Hannah felt that Paul might never have drowned.

Albra, for her part, couldn't help hating her mother. It was there, she saw, in the woman's eyes. The way her mother stopped to frown as if Albra had come to dinner in the boy's clothing. In the beginning, Hannah had run off to cry whenever she walked in the room. But it was the others too; even her sisters sometimes wept at the sight of Albra. Only her father, it seemed, could stand to look at his youngest daughter.

"It's nothing you can help," he would say.

And she would wish he was wrong.

Seasons came and went, and the family did not change toward her; their tense smiles brushed her back into the safety of her room. She dreaded the forced civility of family meals. But when she went down to eat, Albra resurrected the smile they wanted to see, the one which helped their digestion. It offered just enough space between her own lips for the nourishment necessary to go on.

This was during the day.

At night, Albra lay trembling and bruised inside. Alone in the darkness she felt widowed, and in the morning she woke to winter's false light, her body shivering with the sweat of demons. It haunted her still, his memory. It was there waiting in her bed at night. The dream was always the same—her body caught beneath the train, the iron wheels severing her limbs one at a time until only the head was left. At the end of the dream she could look back over the strewn pieces of her body. Then, at the last moment, the head would roll away and the face would be Paul's.

It was there, in that dream of being cut to pieces and left for someone else, that Albra turned to painting. As the season of death melted into the hopeful puddles of April, Albra found in the lengthening days a new presence below the surface of her grief. She passed through spring and early summer brooding over jars of paint as though each contained a revelation. Then one day, she veered off from one of her vague landscapes and painted a canoe. It shocked her. She had never thought there might be a canoe inside her, let alone a lake or a cabin. A release occurred in this crude thing, and that week she painted a summer of canoes.

Albra had found, at last, the edge of herself.

While Hannah was sick, Elizabeth began taking over for her mother. Using the calm tone Calvin preferred at meals, she would comment briefly on the day: a doctor's visit, the rising price of sugar. Laura might speak up too, picking at the edge of her meal with a coffee spoon as she talked, while from upstairs came the faint admonition of Hannah's cough.

When they had finished, Elizabeth took dinner up to her mother while Albra went in to sit with Calvin.

Things, she knew, had gone badly that winter. In church the pews were now clogged with black dresses that fit every woman the same. Listening to her father read aloud from the paper, Albra intuited her own small stake in the nation's anxiety. She felt for it, this country with its grand, imposing mother; its Leagues and Committees and Cabinets all flag-waving their way to patriotic frenzy.

Later, her father would read to her from Homer.

"Whatever happens," he confided, "we've partaken in an

epic good. Even if we are destroyed by it, we will be remembered for what we stood for."

She knew this fact and was proud of it.

War, she realized, was a family affair.

80

In the spring of 1917, Hannah began moving about again. Walking through the house one day, she happened to look in on Albra's room. What she saw made her call out to her husband in alarm.

"Is this why I never see her? She's holed up here making pictures?"

Calvin coughed defensively. "She needed a distraction. I thought something creative . . ."

Albra sat on the stairs listening.

There was a shifting of weight upon the floorboards.

"I don't know," Hannah said. "No one in my family ever painted something like that."

After they had gone, Albra went to her room and shut the door. Kneeling on the floor, she looked for a long while at the paintings in the corner. It was dangerous and thrilling—this new freedom she had discovered—like walking onto a frozen pond. But her mother's words had run like a shuddering crack beneath her feet, and for the first time Albra realized that it could all give way beneath her.

Then all at once, a look of revelation opened across her face. Beneath the pain that had encompassed her life, Albra had unknowingly grown powerful in her ruthlessness. She knew, of course, what it had meant to push aside her brother, to forsake him for her own survival. But until now, she had not realized she could do it again.

That afternoon, Albra worked ferociously in her room, the paint running beneath her brush like blood.

Two things happened to the family that summer: Elizabeth became engaged, and Eddie was wounded.

Elizabeth's engagement had been delayed until Hannah was able to partake in its celebration, in part because the attachment would never have occurred without her need for medical attention. Left as she was to run the home during the day, Elizabeth found herself consulting on a regular basis with her mother's physician. During his weekly visits to the Creighton home, Dr. Julius Leigh was notably drawn to his patient's eldest daughter.

It was a particularly warm evening when the family learned of Elizabeth's engagement. Albra clapped impulsively, forgetting herself for a brief instant. Laura spilled gravy across the tablecloth, only to be miffed when no one noticed. Calvin went on eating after offering his congratulations. Hannah wept, while Julius Leigh did his best to look collected.

"Lizzie! A marriage! How wonderful after all that we've been through. Calvin, isn't that marvellous? Did you know of this? Of course, yes. You must have. And you didn't tell me?"

Calvin reached under the table for his napkin. "It wasn't mine to tell, dear," but no one was listening.

"Forgive me," taking the napkin her husband offered. "My daughter—Mrs. Julius Leigh. It even sounds wonderful . . ."

That night Calvin lay awake for several hours, frowning with a sense of dread that was as hard for him to disown as a son-in-law. He had read of Eddie's injury several weeks before in the paper, slotted like cordwood among a list of casualties. Such lists appeared regularly in the city paper, and Calvin had searched each of them with restrained anxiety ever since his son had arrived in France.

Eddie had been wounded, this much was confirmed by the paper, but Calvin knew almost nothing else. His few contacts in the government were of little use, and the papers could only provide rough generalities. And so Calvin spent a month waiting for the military bureaucracy to report on the fate of his son, keeping what he knew from his wife and daughters until it had been confirmed.

Something had been extinguished inside him that night on that lake with the crowd cornering him at the end of the dock. His guilt had grown in him like a tumour, and in the end he all but blamed himself for Paul's death. But when his oldest son declared he wanted to fight, Calvin had eagerly taken him to enlist. Seeing Eddie march along Front Street with the other recruits had reawakened in Calvin a dormant hope for something pure, and for a time he was happy again. Yet, just as the War had rejuvenated Calvin, it now crushed him with the same indifference that it had dealt with his remaining son. At first he had been too shocked for grief, but gradually the terrible truth began to strangle the ideals on which he had built his life.

Calvin had been meticulous with his instructions and the bootlegger obeyed cheerfully, knowing it meant a larger fee. The bottles were kept locked in Calvin's desk, and with them he drew himself back from the precipice of his despair, unaware of the ground already crumbling beneath his feet. Muttering to himself in his study, Calvin would drink until the courage to be angry returned. All the time he looked for answers to a world that no longer made any sense. By the summer of 1917, Calvin would read Homer for the last time.

On summer evenings, the Creighton family sat together on the front porch where they could avoid the heat lingering inside the house. Hannah sat mending as she liked to in the evening, her feet propped on a stool while her two older daughters played cards at a fold-out table. Calvin smiled absently at his family, sinking into the nearest chair.

"I don't know how you stand the heat in your office," Hannah greeted him. "Lizzie suggested sending you something cold, but I saw you took a glass up with you."

Her husband looked down at his hands, and when he looked up again his voice was almost intimate. "I enjoy having some time to be alone with my thoughts."

"What thoughts are these?" she said, trying to sound coy, the way her daughters could.

Calvin frowned, something in his eyes withdrawing. "There are things you don't need to know. Business has been taking all my time, and there . . . well, there's a war on you know. There are people dying every day. Lives are being ruined. You remember the Elliotts, for instance? Their boy Jack was killed."

Somewhere over the tops of the homes came the low rally of thunder, and from the trees birds called out with anticipation. Calvin still stared at his hands, trying to regain the pleasant numbness. He searched his pockets for a cigar but found none. The earth had turned upside down, it seemed, and yet each day he came home to find everything unchanged. It was Hannah he saw now—sitting like a cork in a bottle, happily knitting away while below her the very ground ached to explode.

Calvin shook his head, suddenly exhausted.

He was drunk, Hannah saw. But at least he cared for the children.

As if reading her thoughts, Calvin looked up abruptly and made an effort to grin. "Where's the young artist?" he asked.

Hannah rolled her eyes. "Fooling with those paints you gave her. You must do something about it, or I shall take it into my own hands."

Calvin sighed, too tired for confrontation. "I don't see any harm in it."

"I draw the line at ignoring family," she continued. "The way you would have it we'd never set eyes on the—so there you are!"

Albra stepped out on the verandah.

"I was just discussing your behaviour with your father, and we're of the opinion that you are spending far too much time with that doodling you do up there. I won't have my daughter coming out funny."

"Funny?" Calvin looked up. "What is that?"

Hannah glared over her glasses. "You know perfectly well what I mean!"

Albra took a deep breath. She had known this would come, ever since her mother first saw her paintings.

Laura smirked into her lemonade. "You have nothing to worry about. Albra has never shown the slightest indication of a sense of humour."

Ignoring her sister, Albra took a rehearsed step toward her mother.

"I have come to ask a favour."

Caught off guard, Hannah leaned back instinctively, placing the needle between her and the child.

"From me?"

"Yes, Mum," laying particular stress on the final word.

Hannah took off her glasses. "What do you want?"

"I need your help," Albra pursed her lips. "I would like to paint you."

The needle fell silently at their feet. "What do you mean?"

"I want to paint your picture."

"When?"

"Would tomorrow be alright?"

"Tomorrow?"

Albra bent over the fallen needle. "Here you are," handing it back to her, point first.

છ

The envelope was on Calvin's desk with the other mail when he came home one evening. A chaplain from Florence wrote to inform the father of Lieutenant Edward C. Creighton that his son had been wounded in action. Edward would, God willing, live. He would also be coming home.

Calvin waited until everyone had gathered for dinner.

Coming downstairs, he mentally noted with annoyance that Julius Leigh would be joining them.

At his chair he paused, nodding a welcome to Julius.

"I have news," his voice suddenly hollow. "News of Edward."

The table became silent.

It was one of those moments that seem to stretch, as though Time itself was pausing to remember the world before altering it forever.

There was crying, of course, followed by the phrases of consolation and assurance Calvin had rehearsed. "After all," he exclaimed with real conviction, "the boy is coming home to us. How many other families can say this?"

"That's true," Hannah whispered. "That's a blessing we must not overlook."

But soon the shock returned and the family sunk beneath their grief. There were questions, of course, spoken across the table to people with no more idea of what was happening than those who asked them. This went on for nearly an hour before anyone noticed Calvin was no longer there.

"Surely he didn't leave us," Hannah exclaimed, seeing already that he had.

In January, Eddie finally wrote and, though he mentioned nothing of being wounded, he sounded much like his old self. This brought a quiet consolation to the family, though also impatience and anxiety. Only Elizabeth had dared detract from their relief.

"It's a hopeful letter," she murmured. "Only . . ."

Albra had watched her father stiffen. "Only what?"

"Well, it's not his handwriting."

Hannah stood suddenly, her knitting falling to the floor.

"Sometimes, Lizzie, you can be such a stupid girl!"

From then on the family spoke of nothing but good things.

Albra smiled to herself, balancing a thought on her lip. It was not very good, to be sure, but there was something of a resemblance. There was struggle here, between the paint and her eye. But there was authority too, and with it Albra saw she had forced her mother to release the grip she still had on her.

In a single arc of red paint she drew a sphere, trapping her mother inside. Then the brush slid beneath the chin in a minute act of revenge. She almost winced as the paint ran like a blade over the pigments of flesh and shadow, cutting her mother open and drawing back the flesh.

Albra shuddered with terrible relief. The canvas, she saw, had its own violence. She had chosen this moment, embracing its inevitability that day on the porch. It had become as unavoidable to her as Paul's death.

"You are doing me a great favour," she said to the fidgeting woman.

"You must have a mind given to detail; it's taken so long. You get that from your father."

"I know. I'm sorry. I thought the whole thing was finished until you sat down and suddenly it was all wrong."

"You're being dramatic. Do what everyone else does— leave out the details and call it impressionistic." Hannah laughed at her own cynicism. "Listen to me. I sound like your father."

"Not to worry," Albra declared suddenly. "I'm done."

"Truly?"

Albra looked at the painting. It was nowhere close probably, but it had served its purpose.

Hannah sighed, pausing in front of the girl. The painting was obviously rough and unprofessional. The difficulty lay in the body mostly, the two-dimensional handling of it, and an extraordinary gauntness around the waist. It made Hannah shudder, and she turned away noting that the dresser needed dusting.

"You're quite earnest for your age."

"The world looks quite earnest from where I stand."

When the door closed Albra placed the painting in her closet to dry.

"There," she hissed. "Now I've got you."

With Eddie gone, Calvin had come to feel isolated among his family. And so it was that he turned to his youngest daughter for company, remembering the easy sympathy they had shared on canoe trips. Since buying Albra her first set of paints, Calvin had been supportive of her artistic interests. That winter he took Albra to see a former employee of his named Arthur, who worked with a group of other artists from a run-down house in the older end of the city.

Arthur met them at the door, and as he showed them upstairs they passed two men arguing in the hallway.

"Forgive my friends," their host muttered. "We don't stand on ceremony here."

The man opened a door at the top of the stairs and ushered them into his studio. "As you no doubt know," turning to look at Albra, "your father has the eye of an artist, but the heart of a banker."

Albra smiled a little shyly.

Arthur's loft was not what she thought of as a studio, but rather an anxious collection of smeared paint and scraps of paper. Along the far wall leaned several finished canvases.

Stepping over a chipped plate she squeezed past her father and stood in a pane of afternoon light. A crust of bread ground beneath her shoe, and looking down, Albra saw the crumbs slip between the floor boards. She looked over her shoulder at her father, who seemed politely oblivious to the surroundings.

Turning from Calvin, Arthur watched the girl poking about his things.

"You're offended." It was said plainly, and without slight.

She looked at him just as frankly. "Yes."

"What would you do differently?"

"I might sweep now and then."

"Perhaps you will have your own studio one day and I'll come and marvel at your floors."

She looked at him defiantly, forgetting her father's shadow by the door. "Maybe I will."

Arthur paused to smile, and it disarmed her.

Rolling up his sleeve, he walked over to the easel where she stood. Then, glancing at her, he returned to painting.

He had a thin hand, she noticed, watching his tendons working beneath the skin.

"Your father says you paint."

Albra was surprised to find she was not embarrassed by this. "That's right."

"Are you good at it?"

"I've stopped painting the typical things, if that's what you mean."

"Done with ponies and sunflowers, are you?"

Glancing up, Albra saw her father inspecting the canvases at the back of the room.

"Don't think you can patronize me," she whispered. "Not even in front of him," nodding toward her father.

His brush faltered in mid-stroke and he turned to look directly at her. "Sorry. Habit."

He painted quietly for a few moments, and the loft became

silent except for the creak of boards behind them. When he finally spoke again, it was almost a whisper.

"What are you painting at the moment?"

"My mother."

Arthur grinned wryly. "Just what the world needs: another angry painter."

"Aren't you cold up here?" Calvin suddenly broke in. "Don't you have any heat? Look, I can see my breath for goodness sake."

"Heat?" Arthur looked up wistfully. "Who can afford heat this time of year?"

"You should come back to work then," Calvin half-joked. "You could live a decent sort of life."

Arthur laughed, scratching thoughtfully at a loose board with his toe.

"If only I wanted to be the decent sort."

"Then maybe you could buy your own house with more room for your things."

"And my painting would become what? A hobby?"

"What's so wrong with that?"

"What would be the point of a larger studio?"

They left shortly after, without Arthur showing them to the door.

"I expect you remember how you came in," he had muttered, before turning back to the easel.

On the street, Albra was pressed to keep up with her father.

"He seems a rude sort," she offered.

Calvin grunted into his scarf. "He gets moody now and then. Tries to be offensive. When he does, I just leave."

They stopped at the corner to let an automobile pass. Albra came up beside her father just in time to speak. "Does he give lessons?"Calvin waited until they reached the far curb before stopping.

"You want lessons?"

"You said I could." She had been hoarding this patiently at the back of her mind.

"Why him?"

She looked up to face him. "He's good."

Calvin laughed and turned again, walking into the wind that caught up his words like last summer's leaves.

"I'll ask him," he said. And just then, his voice seemed warmer than it ever had before.

They met twice a week. For these occasions, Hannah relinquished the front parlour with the promise from Arthur that paint would not touch her floor. Albra began the lessons by showing Arthur what she had done.

After looking at her paintings carefully, he turned to her. "You understand that by being frank I am endeavouring to treat you seriously. You must understand that all praise is irrelevant. This is the first rule of any art. The second is that pain is a symptom of growth. If you are too thin-skinned for this, then I will still teach you, but at the end of a day I will go to your father and collect my money and you will be the same mediocre painter you are at this moment. Which approach would you prefer?"

Albra flinched noticeably at his directness.

"You do not answer," he noted. "Why?"

"I'm just a little taken aback by your—"

"Honesty?" he interrupted.

Albra set her jaw. "Your lack of tact."

Arthur frowned. "Tactful art is of no more consequence than wallpaper. You might as well go back to sunflowers."

"I suppose you don't approve of Van Gogh?"

"He has been gutted by popular affection."

"What's wrong with that?"

"Popularity is the double of contempt. Our society does not admire anything it does not wish to consume. Take Cezanne and Monet, for instance. We revere them, make prints and write articles. They are swallowed by commerce. Their work is nailed to every respectable wall in Europe. We dissect each work as though studying some unfortunate corpse, all in the name of worship. Don't let this fool you. In the sleeve of every disciple is a knife, and every convert is a Judas. Those who sell out to popular opinion know this. That is why we can despise them and love them at the same time. To be immortalized is to embrace perpetual destruction."

"Then why do it?"

Arthur paused, smiling blandly. "It is better than being ignored."

"I used to think you were the happy sort."

"Really?" This seemed to amuse him. "Most of the time I feel rather dull."

"You mean like my painting?"

"Nothing here is dull. Merely undiscriminating."

"Half the time I don't even know what I want to paint."

"Be careful. It's not just what you paint, but how. You must learn to adapt the paint with new methods in order to find yourself. Don't be afraid to fail. A young voice—even of genius—will always begin roughly, and in its roughness will discern the bedrock of its own identity."

Albra laughed, cutting him off at the height of his sermon.

"What's the matter?"

"You even talk like my father."

"Oh dear."

"Is that so bad?"

"He's not terribly discerning in his regard."

"You could do worse in critics."

Arthur suddenly looked her full in the face, annoyed.

"Is your whole family this hostile?"

"Every one of us."

"Don't you take anything seriously? Not even your painting?"

"You have no idea."

"You're wrong there."

"I haven't missed a single opening in two years. My father takes me to them all."

"No," Arthur's hand came up. "That's a mistake. Don't go to any more galleries or smart wallpaper showings. Break free from Cezanne and the Barbizon followers that everyone praises; there is nothing there but the husks of brilliance repeated into obsolescence."

"You're sermonizing again."

"Perhaps you'd like another preacher?"

"Not very good at taking your own medicine, are you?"

"What are you talking about?"

"You might learn to swallow some criticism if you're so set on dishing it out to me. Men are horrible at their own wisdom."

"A suffragette, are you?"

Albra stepped back, her voice suddenly turning haughty. "Probably I am, if I knew what it was."

Arthur shook his head and laughed. "If you want to paint the world, you might think of seeing some of it now and then."

"I have no interest in painting the world, thank you very much. In my opinion, there is far too much of it as it is."

"Have it as you will."

"Don't worry," she said. "I shall."

Calvin put down his glass as Arthur appeared at the door. "How did it go?"

Arthur smiled in spite of himself. "We'll get along."

"So you'll come back?" Calvin felt annoyed after he had spoken, putting it that way.

"Yes. Though you might ask your wife if she would mind not listening by the door."

Calvin could only frown.

That same night at dinner, Hannah openly announced her disapproval. "It's not right," she insisted.

Calvin looked up from his dinner. "What's that?"

"These silly lessons."

Annoyed, Hannah watched as her husband placed this thought among his potatoes, mulling it over in his mouth.

"How so?"

"It doesn't seem odd to you?"

"Not at all. Arthur was quite pleased with her I think." He spoke for Albra's benefit.

"Is that his name? I won't even tell you what I think of him."

"I think you just did."

Hannah grew red. She hated it when he treated her like this. Like a fool. If only he took less, she would let him have so much more.

The whole thing left an uncomfortable sensation in Hannah's stomach, like eroding sand. Since her husband had hung the picture of Albra in their bedroom, Hannah had become aware of something new that threatened her world.

"It's so odd, her being in that room all the time scribbling away. What are other girls her age doing? And now you encourage her with these silly lessons! You go about deciding the girl's life without even consulting her mother. I said nothing when you persuaded Edward to enlist, and look how that has turned out!"

Calvin flinched noticeably. The rest of the family sat frozen, staring at their plates.

"The girls are mine to turn out properly, Calvin. She's not a boy! You keep away from her or she'll be warped by it."

Calvin stood up. "You mean like her brother was?"

The resulting uproar lasted almost half an hour, longer than any conversation they had ever had. By the end of their argument, Calvin and Hannah stood panting at opposite ends of the table, while between them their children sat with martyred composure.

"Then ask the girl!" Calvin bellowed, desperate for resolution. "Let her decide what she wants." Turning on his daughter, Calvin forced the question on Albra. "What do you want? The lessons or not? Out with it."

Albra sat shocked, each parent's gaze bearing down on her.

So this is how it happens, she thought. This is how to do it, and she made a clucking sound with her tongue like cracking egg shells.

"Don't stall," her father nearly shrieked, strained as he was with frustration.

Albra sat up defiantly. "Sorry, Mum," she said, pronouncing each syllable with unneeded emphasis. Her voice suddenly cold and detached, like her father's.

ഇ

Eddie Creighton returned to Canada with two medals, a suitcase and one leg. For the family standing on the platform, it was a moment they had long imagined. But when they finally saw him each uttered a quick gasp. It was not, most of them saw, as bad as it could be. Certainly they had all seen worse.

Eddie got off the train slowly, his body balancing in a way that already looked like habit. As Calvin stepped forward, he was surprised when his son shook with his left hand. Glancing down he saw the right one was now only a stump that attached to a crutch with a steel hook.

"Here," he murmured, taking his son's baggage tag. "I'll get your luggage."

"Dear Eddie," Elizabeth leaned forward to kiss her brother. "We're so glad you're back."

Eddie was mostly quiet, returning the disturbed affection of his family with a fixed smile.

"You can't imagine how I've missed you all," he said.

His words started Hannah crying and everyone instinctively helped her to the car, even Eddie.

That evening after dinner, the photographer Calvin had hired arrived to take a family portrait. Though no one knew it at the time, this was to be a portentous photograph for the family. It captured one of those delicate hesitations that life brings, in which, for a brief instant, everything returns to a moment of innocence and simplicity. In the photograph one may discern the faces not yet arrived, and those shortly to leave; one may finger the preserved wedding invitation, then so recently printed, the certificates of birth and death still unthought of. There is more here than the awkward smiles of a family now dead.

four

There were no clothes: the two had been buried as they were born.

Gravediggers had removed the last nuisances of wealth from hands and teeth, so that years later, when the coffin collapsed under the weight of an invading root, little would remain of Beatrice Mead and her nameless child. When the worms had done with the lingering traces of flesh and cartilage, the two would finally lie at rest, child fused to mother in earth.

Six feet above them, Gabriel stood to one side while his mother prayed.

The hushed sound of her voice disappeared among the stones. Mary still came here occasionally, drawn to the dead woman by something deeper than sympathy.

Gabe glanced about uneasily, wishing he had not come. In the branches above him, a sparrow called. A breeze ran through the trees, and for an instant, he closed his eyes to let it drift over him. Between two stones, beads of dew hung from a spider's web, heavy and pregnant as pearls. Glancing at his hands, he noticed the stain of dark sepia beneath his nails, and from where he stood, he saw his mother's head bent low as it had been the day before.

They brought the birds home from the market, taking them to the bathroom where Mary cut off the heads. Kneeling beside the tub, she leaned forward and slid her knife above the breast, jerking it upwards with a rapid sawing motion.

He watched her hands as she killed each bird, the way they held their protesting limbs against the cold iron of the tub, pinning their necks with her thumb.

It was Gabe's job to take the dead birds to the kitchen where Mona held them in a pot of boiling water. Her face glistened with sweat as she worked in the steam and stench of wet feathers. Then, picking them out by the feet, she took each one to the backyard to hang on the clothesline. When all the birds were boiled, Gabe and Mona plucked the feathers from them.

Two cats appeared at the side of the house.

As he worked, Gabe's hands became slippery with blood and the grease that oozed from the sockets. The children next door gaped at him over the fence. It was hot and his head began to ache. Flies circled about his hands.

When he was done, he took the birds he had plucked back into the kitchen. He waited uncomfortably as his mother bent over the carcasses, drawing out the organs and intestines in handfuls all blue and yellow.

But on the last one Mary stopped suddenly, her hand deep within the bird's body. As she withdrew her arm, the strain on his mother's face evaporated and she held up a small egg between her fingers.

It would only be later, when he was much older, that Gabe would understand what his mother felt. But there, at that moment, the little egg appeared perfect—all red and still warm—like a rose in bud, waiting to open.

It was summer, and even death looked beautiful.

When she was done, he went to the bathroom to clean up. The severed heads looked up at him from the bottom of the tub, their eyes stupid with shock.

Making sure no one was looking, he examined one hesitantly. The remaining feathers were stiff and matted with dried blood, but the little beak opened as he pried it with his finger. He wondered at it, this thing that had so recently been alive. He could not help remembering the jet of hot blood as their flesh yielded to the knife, the little heads rolling about the drain, gazing back at the lifeless spasms of their own bodies.

Just then he heard someone on the stairs and quickly tossed the thing in a pail with the others. He took it out to the backyard and dumped them near his compost pile. At the gate, he turned back to see the two cats fighting over one of the heads.

As she finished her prayer, Mary paused for a moment to look upon the tomb of Beatrice Mead and her child. At her feet she noticed a worm, fat and happy with itself, weaving a silver tangle of mucus in the grass.

Without thinking, she pushed her heel into it. Then, lifting her foot, she saw it had been transformed, the dark flesh peeled back like petals from a flower.

ॐ

The orange haze of a July afternoon sat heavily on the porch of Miss Pross's boarding house. As the afternoon dragged, the sun settled on a group of men pinched together on a porch swing. They sat in pious stillness, like an Orthodox display of icons, only a shirtless man in the middle moving now and then to knock stubs of ash from his cigar. A boy rode by on a red bicycle, carelessly ringing the bell as he went.

No one stirred as the front door opened and a man crossed the porch and walked into the street. Here he braided his way through the people enjoying the summer heat. In doorways and about shop fronts hung a collection of tramps, charlatans, vagrant whores, and returned soldiers still awed at being alive.

"Like a circus," Gopnik muttered, stumbling over the tranquil legs of a drunk.

Individually, these people were of no consequence to him; they were like seeds silenced beneath the asphalt of commerce. But together they gave off a restless odour that kept him from dissolving into the dust and shadows. He was tacitly accepted among them, and shared their jaded integrity. In these people, Gopnik found the unsettled energy so necessary to his reality.

There was some confusion ahead and, as Gopnik approached, he saw a cart overturned in the street and people gathered about in great commotion. A milk cart had tipped over on the road and people were pushing at each other, trying to catch up some of the liquid as it pooled and tapered in the cracks of the street. To break free from the throng, Gopnik stepped up on the axle of the broken cart and a dark smile passed across his face before he jumped down and carried on.

Stopping at a corner, he searched in his shirt pocket for a cigarette. Gopnik looked across the road to where another man stood in front of a shop window. He glanced up at Gopnik, scarcely nodding before turning back to the window.

Gopnik turned into a doorway where he followed a set of stairs up three floors. At the landing, he passed a woman who sat feeding an infant in the hallway.

She seemed unperturbed by Gopnik's presence, looking up from her breast only long enough to nod.

"You're late," she said.

He knocked before entering a door at the end of the hall-way. In the centre of the room, a group of men sat in a small circle. The windows were opened wide and those sitting about were already wiping away sweat from their faces.

Gopnik nodded at each man individually, greeting them in turn. "Hello, Comrade, hello."

Soon came the sound of feet in the hall; the door opened and the man Gopnik had seen across the road sat down.

"All clear," he said.

A sickly-looking man in a suit jacket nodded and turned to the others.

"Gentlemen, thank you for coming. You will please forgive the humidity."

At this he paused to glance at Gopnik who shifted uncom-fortably in his chair.

"Having so . . . so candidly spoken his mind last week, I would like to start this meeting by replying to Comrade Gopnik with what I hope may be seen to be a more tempered approach to achieving the inevitable restoration of the People's inheritance. I speak, obviously, not for my own partisan agen-da but for what I see to be the good of the Party and the People."

Throughout this speech, Gopnik stared at the floor.

"I support my fellow worker's assertion that we must break our silence to the People. Despite the dangers this may bring from the present government, the People will rally to us. Of this there can be no doubt, for we represent the interest of the working man, and where better for him to put his heart?" He paused here to wipe away the sweat from his face. "Having resolved to present this nation with its destiny, we have now only to decide how. Surely if the capitalists have shown us anything it is that war—like the one so thankfully over—brings only atrocity. The losses our people have incurred have taught us that violence will only breed unnecessary violence, and while the capitalists must know that we are not hesitant to apply force if provoked, the People must see that the Party brings the promise of peace and justice to a nation crippled by exploitation and exhausted by war. Would the People even respond to a party that preached violence, after all that our sons have seen in Europe? Have we not had a stomach full of this mindless waste and attrition?"

Now pale and sweating from his oration, the man paused to survey those seated around him. Several of the men nodded resolutely, and the speaker took a deep breath before starting again.

"It is therefore, Comrades, my feeling that prudence and success lie for us through political, rather than military, confrontation. Let us take our message to the streets. Let us take it to the People; to their homes and in their factories. Let the Party's name ring in their ears! What have we to fear from the capitalists' flawed electoral system? It is they who will be afraid as we beat them at their own game! Can the corpulent burden of the rich pose any legitimate threat to the People's might? I say: Not on your life!"

Ending at an emotional height, the man fell backward into his chair in a fit of coughing. When he had quieted, one of the men handed him a handkerchief.

Gopnik eyed each one of them in turn, shaking his head.

"Spoken like a true bureaucrat, I thought. Look at you—wearing a jacket here in this heat!"

"If I . . ." the man almost choked. "If I deem it appropriate to show my reverence for the formality of these proceedings by wearing my Sunday best, it's of no concern to you, Comrade Gopnik!"

Gopnik stood, spitting across the floor. "Have you learned nothing from our Soviet brothers? Do you think they could have toppled a tsar through negotiation? Hah! You must be tired; go back to your dream. How long have I been recruiting support?" He slapped the man beside him as though presenting evidence. "Support based on promises we've made. Promises of change—of revolution. If the Slavs can do it, why can't we? You said we needed support before action. Well, I say the People will follow action. No; don't sputter away, John, like some broken horse. Three years ago you were ready to slit throats. Now you want to cut a deal."

So heated did the sickly man become now that he again broke into a fit of coughing and shaking. "We must still remain truthful to the laws of a higher order, man. Don't forget we must all answer to God."

"God?" Gopnik scoffed at the pale man mercilessly. "My boss counts each drop of sweat that runs off my back, and you want us to rely on God? For what? Your soul? Oh, you'll be allowed that alright. It's the capitalists' one generosity. But our bodies and all they produce are given up to the owners. Don't you see? The church is only the final element of the capitalists' exploitation. We would never have Sundays off if they weren't sure the church would direct your minds away from the wrongs done to us in this life. Go to church? Sure you can go. Take your wife, too, so that when she complains about your lot you can remind her of the inheritance she has bought with dutiful suffering. Well, wake up lads and look about you! The meek haven't inherited anything, so if we want a piece of this earth it'll be up to us to take it. No one is going to hand it to us. We're to earn it like men. And those that want to go pray, well go ahead. But you'll not be touching my share if you won't fight for it beside me!"

One of the other men shook his head at Gopnik. "Have you had your head in the ground? Haven't you seen the suffering that comes with all your grand ideas?"

"You talk to me of suffering? Have you not looked around your own neighbourhood? At your fellow workers? What's

their lot? If I didn't know where you worked I might be looking for a job in your bed of roses! But I see your kids coming
home each day, so I know you're hurting same as the rest of
us."

This brought the man to his feet. "What're you saying?"

Sensing the danger here, Gopnik stepped forward until
their noses nearly touched. Then, in a sympathetic whisper, so
the rest could barely hear: "You know I ain't saying anything
like that Matthew. You know I've nothing but respect for you
family men. Don't know how you do it. But I see that you too
know difficulty, and it grinds in me like my own hunger."

Gopnik turned then to face the others. "You can't tell me
that all we've to do is walk up there to that new parliament in
Ottawa and take power. It ain't going to be that easy,
Comrades. Though there has been suffering, it has been done
for the capitalists' prosperity. If the People want to taste their
own victory then they will have to fight for it; mark my words,
lads. And those that can't bear to suffer again, well for them
it'll be too bad. I sympathize with them. I do. But there is a
larger good to be won, and personal sacrifice must soon
become commonplace if it is to be obtained. You want peace—
course you do. But do you have it now? Can you have peace
inside you when someone's stealing the bread from your table?
Ain't we all in a state of siege every day of our lives? And
won't we be there until someone stops the thieving? I've heard
words tonight like atrocity and violence. But I ain't heard no
one mention a thing of justice, or liberty . . . why's that? Is it
because deep down we all find those things a little too frightening? Ain't that what it is? Don't you just wish the bad things
would go away—and when they won't, when you get older,
don't you find that you can live with them? My old man was
like that. I know those thoughts myself. But now and then I see
those faces in one of them nice new cars go by, or see one of
them women all dressed up who looks right through you. And

it's then, lads, that the anger in me stands up and I say, No! No, I can't go on this way, only working and subsisting. Ain't that what we all do? Don't you ever get to thinking there's more? More than cans of Clark's soup and smuggled beer? Lads, I don't mind working for a living. But I damn well want to own my labour, what I make, if I'm gonna struggle so."

John had taken off his jacket, which seemed to relieve him. "You speak moving words, Comrade. And I can see your heart is with the People's plight. But I ask you again, can violence bring anything other than despair and anarchy?"

At this there was a pause. Somewhere beyond the walls a clock ticked. Finally, a heavy man stood up. "I sympathize with your notions," he said, looking Gopnik in the eye. "But I been to war once, and I tell you I ain't going back to it. In two years of butchering and being butchered, I didn't see no good come of it. I'm for trying other means."

Several others nodded their heads.

Standing, Gopnik looked about him. "Ain't no one with me?"

A short silence was his reply.

"Fine! You're all cooked, then, are you? All set to talk but ain't a one of you ready to look the consequences of your ideas in the eye, is there?" Sensing he had lost, Gopnik paused to collect himself, drawing out the awkward silence like a rug beneath their feet. "You all don't know shit. You're talkers, is all. Harmless and annoying—like flies hovering about the rich man's plate. You and your Party ain't never gonna leave this room."

With that Gopnik strode out, leaving his chair upturned on the floor.

The tall man on the bed sat watching the others after Gopnik had left. Taking up his hat from his knee, he stood quietly and looked about him.

"You shouldn't be standing still, not while the whole

world yearns to move forward." His voice hung in the still air of the room like an odour. Turning then, he walked out into the hall in search of Gopnik.

The man was Thomas Oban.

ɞ

Something had come over Earl Pryce in the last few months. Boundaries had begun to erode, compromised by an anxiety that shook his resolution to surmount and conquer. Like a wasting mirror, the reflection of the man had begun to peel away.

For over a year now when he kissed his wife, there was no longer an energy in her touch, no thought of pleasure or seduction. Only the mechanical hunger of conception. Her body frightened him now, mocked him. Never had Pryce suspected the wretchedness, the self-negation, the plaguing suspicion of debility behind the act. Death must follow birth, he thought. And the fingers caressing him suddenly felt like a noose.

What they had both longed for once was no longer theirs. How had this happened? Nakedness had become a state of pain, and he loathed their time together. In its wake came the weakness that he had fought all his life to overcome. It was laced with guilt and an odd sort of hate, and carried the memory of his mother standing over her husband's coffin.

"What will we do, son?" with pleading disability. "What will you do?"

And so he had gone back to the one he had tried to forget, sulking along the street as if returning to a hidden bottle long unneeded. She had been happy to see him, careful between buttons not to ask about his wife. He couldn't help but grin when she smoothed his hair and called him Early Bird, whispering in that voice. Then, in that room with its echoes, Pryce tried to rediscover something that had never been his in the first place but only a repulsive need that drove him on to destroy and plunder until all of him was reduced to a single act of currency.

Stepping into the darkness of the street, Earl walked quickly, noting the smell of ore in the air that blew up from the harbour. His feet sounded severe and unrelenting against the street, and his mind wandered instinctively to the mill. Even his own breath seemed distant in the emptiness of the street, and from the curtainless windows above him came the muffled cry of children.

Penny Pryce and her husband had always been happiest when driving. Earl had bought a new Roadster after the War. Unlike most people, he had never been afraid of the new power and speed of automobiles. Since first owning a car, Earl loved driving with the top down to let the wind and sun rush about him. Penny also looked forward to driving. It was the only place they could talk anymore.

"You saw the doctor today?"

"Yes."

"How was it?"

"No change."

They drove for a while in silence, clouds passing over head.

"I stopped by to see Jean and Michael afterward."

"And how were they?"

"Mike says we must run up to town for the night. But I suggested they come out to us in the country instead. It's so much nicer here."

"Will they come?"

Penny's gaze trailed off across the fields of browning grain. "They're free this weekend . . ."

Earl squeezed his wife's hand. "Make it a Saturday night, would you? You know what I'm like at the end of the week."

"We could put them up in the room with the east gable, but I don't think there's enough room for the cot."

"Has she got him sleeping on the floor now?"

"Well, they won't come without the child now will they? And it's not as though we own a crib . . ."

Earl stared at the road.

"Earl?"

The car turned down one of the country roads that branched off the one leading into the city. "Shall we take a drive along the lake?"

"Alright."

It was almost evening and all around them the land was still. Grass and corn stood as motionless as the fence posts that reclined into the pink glow of setting light. Bales of barley and oats were scattered across hills. Dogs sat in the dust and gravel of laneways.

They came to the lake. Hugging the shoreline, Pryce stared fixedly on the road while his wife gazed out at the expanse of water. There were no shadows now, only the cool wind off the lake. Penny removed her hat to let the wind pass through her hair. He looked at her, admiring the declining light against her neck.

"Slow down!"

The car squeezed to the far edge of the road to avoid a row of black carriages.

"What are they doing here?"

Past the carriages, a group of people stood about in the sand. The women wore white bonnets to restrain their hair, while the faces of the men were lost in the shadow of large-brimmed hats.

"What're they doing?" Earl repeated.

"I think they're courting!"

Scattered along the beach walked three or four couples. They stood firm and solid against the blurred horizon of water and sky. Everything in black and white.

"Talk about the dark ages."

"I think it's sweet."

"To be that backward?"

Penny waved and one of the girls, tall and pretty in a dress of blue flowers, waved back at them. Earl sped up as soon as they were past, and the car disappeared in a roar of dust. "I hear they have families of ten or twelve. Can you imagine?"

"No." Penny sat back into the seat. A sound of anguish buried in the engine's roar.

His palms became slippery along the steering wheel. "There are other options for us," he said into the wind.

Penny was quiet for a long time before answering. "I only want one."

"There's a woman I've heard of and, for a fee, of course, she will get us in . . ."

Penny stared at him through the wall of passing air. "You cannot buy one."

"The families often can't afford it themselves."

"So it's charity then?"

"I suppose."

"For whom?"

Earl paled.

"Well, go right ahead. But you'll have to find another mother."

"What do you want from me?" he yelled.

Penny was silent, staring out at the lake.

"If I order it the men who work for me can build anything."

"That doesn't help me."

The car skidded to a sudden halt, and the two were enveloped in a fog of grey dust.

"What do you mean by that?"

"Just what I said."

"I know what you meant!"

His wife looked at him.

Earl didn't move. The dust had settled now. Husband and wife stared at one another.

"It's not my fault, dammit."

"Fine. Now will you start driving, or shall I get out and push?"

"You don't understand," he whispered. "It isn't my fault." But the engine was racing again, and his voice was lost in a groan of metal.

∞

The problems between Mary and Thomas were only exacerbated by time. Their marriage was now held together by necessity and obligation, and the tension between them left the family divided. Mary, always remote and exacting, now had bouts of suffocating tyranny. Thomas, on the other hand, had grown more distant, as if countering his wife's omnipresence in the family. Despite their own estrangement, each remained dedicated to the child closest to them. Furious that Hal had left to fight in France, Mary turned all her attention to her youngest son.

If life had not embraced Gabriel Oban it had at least accepted him, and in the following years he had grown like a northern pine, doggedly clinging to the bedrock of his physical existence. He spent most of his time in the garden now, where, among the brute delicacies of rotting matter, he tended the union of death and life within the soil. Its mystery was not lost on him, and he watched as the green shoots protruded from the dark mass of old peels and eggshells.

One afternoon Gabe was startled to look up from the row

he was weeding to find his father standing by the gate, looking at him.

"Need some help with that?" the man asked, nodding at the upturned earth.

For the first time since he could remember, Gabe smiled at his father without effort. "Sure."

Taking the hoe from the boy, Thomas drove it into the dark soil, breaking up the roots and tendrils of weeds as he went.

Gabe watched, slightly awed, as the man worked.

"You know," Thomas said, glancing at the boy over his shoulder. "I started at the mill shovelling slag. That was heavy work," smiling distantly at the shaft of the hoe. "Feeding the ovens all day."

Gabe moved to the next row and began to pull the weeds with his hands. "Why not get an easier job?"

Thomas shrugged. "It paid well. I had a family to bring here. There had to be some place for us to live. Besides, easy ain't better usually. Just easier."

They were quiet for a moment, each thinking as they worked.

Thomas continued. "I was lonely then, not knowing any-one. The ovens can be good company."

Gabe looked up from the soil. "I know," he said. "It's the same way with a garden."

His father paused from hoeing, and his eyes settled on the humble rows around him. Then, turning to his son, he smiled.

Encouraged, Gabe began telling the man his plans for the garden. "I thought maybe we could plant some apple trees there by the fence. Mahonia knows someone who sells saplings . . ."

Thomas looked at the fence for a moment, trying to visualize what the boy was saying. "Would be a while before you get any fruit."

"That's alright," Gabe said quietly, suddenly unsure of

himself. "I've got lots of time." And then the boy looked up at his father, his voice was almost a whisper.

"You have, too. Don't you?"

Thomas glanced at him, his eyes lingering for a moment on the pale cheek. Then from behind a voice came between them.

"There'll be no fancy orchard along my fence." Mary stood looking at them, her eyes bright and hard. "That's prime soil for turnips or more carrots, perhaps."

Thomas stood very still.

"I need you inside," she said to the boy.

Gabe glanced over his shoulder on his way to the house. Neither of his parents had moved, but now from behind her his father somehow looked cornered and wounded, waiting for the final blow to come.

If there was anything that Gabe recognized in another person, it was loss, and it drew him instinctively now to his father. Consequently, in the days that followed, he was deeply confused as his father suddenly became more remote. One day when his Thomas came home from the mill, Gabe quietly followed him upstairs to his old bedroom where the man still slept.

"There's some ground I'm turning over outside," he said, as a kind of offer.

Turning abruptly, his father shut the door on the boy's voice. "Let me sleep. I been working, not playing about all day in the dirt!"

What the boy couldn't see was that he had become a spoil of the quiet war between his parents. Lines had been drawn in the Oban home that included more than bedrooms, and his father could no more reach out to him than a soldier could approach someone in an enemy trench. Between them now lay a conflict that Gabe neither started nor understood, but which would come to define everything in his life from that time forward.

For Thomas, the disappointment was perhaps as deep as that felt by his son, but he was far less uncertain about its cause. Standing there in the garden, Thomas had glimpsed a shadow of the child he had worked hard to raise but knew little of. Yet because his wife now saw the boy as her own, he had been forced to draw back from the child that reached out to him. That day in the garden, Thomas had come as close to his son as he would ever get.

Despite the absence of his father, Gabe prospered under Mary's wing. Meanwhile, his father's own emotional impoverishment forced him to reach out for affection in other quarters. Now almost nineteen, Mona worked in the office of a machine parts manufacturer while remaining under the paternal eye of Thomas Oban, often using his authority to shield her from the restrictions Mary imposed. In the end, though, the girl always succumbed to Mary's jurisdiction.

But there were gifts. Small traces of luxury dredged up by Thomas from the trunks of street vendors. A little broach with a broken pin, scraps of lace and handsome buttons, even a pocket Bible.

"See there, on the cover? The tiny lamb next to a lion."

"Oh yes. How beautiful. You really shouldn't . . ."

"You deserve more than you got now, that's for sure."

"Aunt Hannah says I've too much thought for myself already, and I wouldn't—"

"Never mind her," Thomas growled. "You make things brighter. You're a light in the darkness, just like a pearl—pink and pure, even in the dark bottom of an ocean."

Thomas and Gopnik had just come off the line at Leda Steel, and on their clothes hung the acrid stench of ore. They turned down a quieter street in the direction of Gopnik's boarding house. When they reached the place, he stopped to talk to a severe-looking woman in a blue apron.

"Oh hello, Miss Pross. I'd like you to meet a friend of mine. I was gonna just sneak up and show him the work I did for you in the attic—if it isn't any trouble that is?"

The woman smiled, warming noticeably at Gopnik's words. "Of course, Mr. Gopnik. He did a fine job there," looking at Thomas. "Hasn't leaked in two years."

Gopnik nodded appreciatively. "Thanks. We won't be long."

Leading Thomas up a narrow staircase, Gopnik paused at the landing to look around. Then, pulling on a rope the two men stepped back as a hatch opened into the ceiling.

"Watch your head; there's some low beams up here."

Thomas was silent as they ascended into the loft. Balancing on two of the crossbeams, Gopnik lighted a match that produced a halo of light about his face.

"This way," he whispered. "In the corner there."

Following the light, Thomas stepped gingerly in the other man's direction. Gopnik handed the match to him.

"It's almost out."

"Then light another."

Squinting as the new match flared, Thomas looked to find Gopnik holding a wad of newspaper the size of a large hornet's nest.

"Not too close, Oban. Keep the light at a distance," he said, peeling away a thick layer of the yellowing paper. "I wouldn't want you to wake up these babies."

Thomas was almost giggling with anticipation. "Whatcha got there?"

"Just a little hope for the People's future." As Thomas held the wad of papers closer to the match, the dim light fell on a stack of long tubes.

"Candles?"

Gopnik laughed. "Yeah, sort of. Though these'll light up a whole neighbourhood."

Thomas's eyes dilated suddenly in the fading light.

"Light another, man."

Thomas's voice came as a gasp. "Why can't you?"

"Are you outta your mind?"

"Yeah, okay. Just a second."

Gopnik reappeared holding the dynamite as a new match was lit, his teeth bright as a row of mirrors.

"Where'd you get them?"

Gopnik chuckled again. "A little memento from my mining career."

"They didn't notice?"

"They noticed too late."

"What're you going to do with them?"

Gopnik wrapped up the newspaper. Though he spoke in a whisper, his voice remained agitated, hardened.

"That's not the question. The question is, when? It has to be soon . . . these babies aren't good forever, you know. They gotta be used. I've been waiting a long time, Oban. Waiting till things were right—like they were against Cataract. I been waiting, and it's time now. Sure people are happy the War's over. But they're pissed too. Those with dead finally see their sons were wasted over there fighting for the capitalists. And now all the guys who knew how bad they were treated are back home. Think of it Oban! Those men don't even blink at a dead body. All them pissed at the government, finding they gotta go back to slugging in a factory the way it was before, maybe worse. And there's no drink either! That's the real clincher. No booze to lose your anger in, the rage'll sit in their bellies until they want to explode. Them soldiers see nothing has changed for all their dying and suffering. It's time. All they need is someone to start the fire, to bring down the walls of oppression and privilege. To get what's theirs."

The match went out, enveloping the two men in darkness.

Thomas sat completely still on one of the beams, his face hidden now. "You can't mean it?"

"The hell I can't. You'll see, Thom. Freedom ain't clean. It ain't all brass bands and flags. There's some who have to get dirty first," his hand came out of the darkness to rest on Thomas's arm. "That's us."

It was a long time before Thomas spoke. "There's my family. I . . . I need some time Goppy. To think this over."

Gopnik sighed, deeply disappointed. "Alright, Thom. I'll give you a little. But then I'm gonna act on my own."

⁑

That summer, Penny and Earl Pryce were happy again. Happier, Earl believed, than they had ever been. Penny was pregnant, finally and incontestably. As soon as it had been confirmed, Earl had insisted they go to church. "To give thanks," he persisted.

"Why not thank me?" Penny said wryly.

Afterwards, they had gone out to lunch in town, but returned early because Penny was not feeling well.

"The doctor told me to expect this," she explained.

When his wife was asleep, Earl went for a stroll in the pasture beside the house. The grass swayed heavily in the afternoon breeze, heads bent low with seed. A cow and her calf stood looking out over the field, chewing together with a look of gratification. Through the breeze came the ardent scratch of crickets.

"Good year for bugs," he mused.

It was not until recently that he had come to recognize the pleasure he received from his farm. Nonetheless, he had decided that Penny would be better off in the city until the child was born.

Earl had been stunned when she first told him. Almost immediately the resentment he felt towards his wife transformed into an uncomfortable veneration, which settled between their lives like a mother-in-law. A giant bouquet was ordered, using so many flowers that people walking by the shop thought someone important had died.

If anything tainted the peace of this time for Penny, it was the distracted expression that had settled on her husband.

"It was nothing," he assured her, "Only some problems at the plant."

When he was a child, Earl had once come home badly beaten by an older boy at school. It was spring, and as he reached the farm, he had seen his father planting in the field. Earl remembered the look in the man's eyes, realizing in that instant that nothing scares a man like shame. When he reached the house his mother had soothed and bathed him, the way he knew she would. Since that day Earl had never appeared shaken or in pain to any man. Only women.

So it was that Earl turned now to Leda Steel.

About mid-summer, Earl became concerned with the growing level of inertia that had settled upon his company at the close of the War. Having ceased her production of munitions, the manufacturing end of Leda Steel had largely gone unused while the bulk of her income again came from the production of steel. Feeling the need to streamline his operation, Earl quickly sold off the manufacturing end of the business to the Steel Company of Canada, and began an extensive critique of Leda's production. Using war-time profits, he upgraded his equipment and, exploiting the surplus of labour among returning soldiers, he managed to hold off the union's push for a wage increase.

In late July, Earl left Penny for several days to tour some of the mills in the northern United States. When he returned, Pryce was full of strained enthusiasm, and as summer drew on he became increasingly fixated on the future of his steel mill. Dinners with his wife were increasingly rare. More often, too, he came home irritated, obsessed with a growing animosity towards those he employed.

"I tell you, if I saw a man looking at my wife the way some of them look at my mill it would be against the law. It all comes down to a handful of radicals," he exclaimed. "Now, south of the border, I met people who knew how to handle that kind. That's what we needed for those bastards in Winnipeg. Thinking they can control production . . ."

ℬ

How Mary Oban broke it to him no one ever remembered. But when Thomas was told he went into a rage like no one had ever seen him, as though some part of the man had snapped under an incredible shock. They purposely kept the girl away from him, and when he couldn't find her, Mary gave him some money, knowing he would drink it. When he left she thought that was the end of it, that he would get over it the way he had other things.

It was Gabe who heard him come in the side door that night, and soon after he was startled by a sudden cry. The boy stumbled into the house, his first thought was that someone had caught a burglar. He was nearly knocked over by his mother at the top of the stairs.

"What is it?" he yelled, still half asleep and out of breath.

But his mother only looked at him with wide, dilated eyes, her hair falling about her. Another scream reverberated through the house, and Mary turned abruptly toward it.

"Mona!" she gasped.

A light was on in the room. For the rest of his life, Gabe never forgot the sight of his father as he punched the girl in the belly. Mona's fingers tore at his face and clothes, but he had her pinned at the neck and her face was nearly purple. Above it all came the roar of Thomas's voice, which shook the boards beneath Gabe's feet.

"Out! Get it out you slut!"

The room sat in ruins: the bed and a dresser were all over-turned and both Thomas and Mona were tangled in an array of sheets and torn clothing. Mary grabbed at the man's arm and he froze suddenly, staring at her hand. Then Thomas seemed to lose his balance and fell onto the bed.

Mary turned to the girl who lay on the floor completely still, her mouth open as though trying to scream.

Gabe looked in awe at the long streak of blood that ran to the bottom of her shift.

Hal appeared at the door. "Is she dead?" he whispered.

A shudder ran through the girl's frame and she began weeping so violently that Gabe could see her sides shaking.

Seeing the girl like this, Mary remembered the body of Beatrice Mead, and she turned and struck savagely at her husband. Then, looking about, Mary grabbed her son by the arm. "Get that man out of here," she hissed.

As the boy spoke, Thomas rose numbly and followed his son out of the room without looking back. When they had gone, Mary whispered something to Hal, who quickly left.

In the kitchen Gabe placed a basin of water before his father. "Your face is cut," he observed in a quiet voice.

Hal returned in a little while with the doctor.

Above them came the sound of voices and furniture being righted, and soon Hal came down again. He paused as he entered the kitchen, and looked for a moment at the back of his father's head.

"You killed it," he said, as though commenting on the weather.

Thomas nodded, looking down at the water cupped between his hands. "Yes."

A hush had fallen on the house, no one wishing to talk for fear of stepping on something that was already broken.

Thomas finally turned to look at his sons.

"I think you should leave," Hal muttered.

Thomas started. "I'm your—"

"All the same you should leave. Until Mona . . . I'll talk to her. Find out who it was. Maybe he'll marry her, and then you could come back."

"Why should he marry her now . . . ?"

The three sat in silence about the table.

"How did this happen?" Thomas finally whispered.

Just then, Mary's voice came from the top of the stairs. "Boys, she called."

Thomas listened to the sound of their feet on the stairs. Alone now, he pushed the basin away and rested his head in both hands. Outside, a dog barked from somewhere far away.

"Oh God," he groaned, sinking to his knees. And as he looked up at the ceiling, his gaze caught on a fly dangling from an abandoned web.

Only a runny stratum of light played in the horizon when Gopnik arrived at Leda Steel the next morning. It had rained all night, and the magenta plume of flame above the exhaust stack gleamed back at him from puddles in the street. Since falling out with the other members of the Party, he had found himself isolated. Without them he had grown irritable, anxious to vent the wrath his temperament hinged on. Normally self-controlled, Gopnik now had bouts of vicious irrationality that left him unable to sleep or eat. Like a rabid animal, he wandered the city looking for something to bite. Crossing the street, Gopnik nodded to a man waiting for his shift to start. He was sitting on the curb, head resting between his arms.

"Hello, friend."

The man stirred and looked up.

Gopnik stepped back. "Thom?"

"Hello Goppy."

"What the hell are you doing here?" Gopnik sat down next to him.

"Smoke?"

"Don't see your lunch."

"Don't have one."

"Not hungry, eh?"

"That's it."

"Well, old Pross made mine with that damn awful meat again . . ."

Thomas attempted to smile. "The rotten stuff?"

Gopnik nodded wryly, pushing out his bottom lip. "Yup. Surprised you can't smell it yourself. I been attracting cats the whole way here."

"That bad, eh?"

"Oh yessiree."

"Not one for waste is she?"

"And with what I pay her too!"

Thomas was quiet for a moment. "What d'ye say we get something later?"

Gopnik smiled to himself. "Sounds good to me."

After that the two sat on the curb in silence, watching other men arrive. When the whistle blew, they stood and went to work.

Later that morning Gopnik found Thomas curled between two ingots. Shielding him as best he could from the eyes of anyone wandering by, Gopnik listened as the man poured out his grief. He told him everything: of his wife keeping herself from him, of the years of shame and anger, and finally of the girl who finished his disgrace by ruining herself.

"You can't believe what I did."

"Do you know who brought her to this?"

Thomas shook his head forlornly. "Some clerk . . ."

Gopnik's eyes narrowed. "One of the managers' little pimps!"

The other man stilled.

"Bet they whooped it up when he told them about it. Bet they giggled their big heads off."

"Who?"

"His bosses, of course. They just love hearing about another one of us getting screwed."

Thomas looked at him.

"Oh yeah. Only they got the best retort there is: 'What, just once? I screw her father every day.'" Gopnik shook his head. "I see you looking angry at me, but that's how it is. Have you forgotten who waited with you while you bought the girl all them presents? I feel for you, I do. But you're getting fucked every day of your life, and I never seen you cry over that."

Thomas shook his head helplessly.

"Thom, don't you see how strong you are? So close to standing on your own two feet, at last. Not like the sheep in there," he nodded over his shoulder toward the ovens. "No. Like a man. Letting no man leave you disgraced. Yeah, what you did was hard. But why'd you do it?"

Thomas shuddered and lowered his stare. "I had to . . ."

"That's right. You had to. You took the hard road, the dirty road. But the right road. I thought such mettle was lost to greed and cowardice but I see now that I am not alone—that I am not the only man willing to suffer for his ideals. Don't judge yourself badly, Thom. History will remember you as a torch to follow. A champion of the People!"

Glancing furtively over his shoulder, Gopnik reached out and touched the man on the arm. "I was not mistaken in you, Thom," his voice lowered to a hiss. "A while ago I offered you a chance to prove yourself. You struggled then and your fears overcame you. But since then you have proven yourself capable of courage and sacrifice. What I need to know is whether you are still willing to pay for those ideals, or are you going to go back on yourself? Will you again bargain for your dignity?"

A long moment of silence hung between the two men as the rain fell around them. Oily pools of water began to swell about their feet. Thomas stood stiffly and pushed the hair back from his face, trying to smile as he did.

ℰ

September 1, 1919 was a wet day in Hamilton. The rain began in the early morning and kept up a sporadic presence throughout the day. The Spectator later blamed poor attendance on the damp weather, though over ten thousand people still came out to the events and demonstrations in both Dundurn and Victoria Parks. Despite their proximity to a booth of Temperance people, several bootleggers peddled their transgression among the crowds. One such man pulled his three daughters about on a wagon, pausing now and then to talk with the men watching the races. When he was approached, the bootlegger quickly pocketed the necessary amount and one of the girls lifted a bottle from beneath her skirt.

"The indignities of free trade," he complained to one man.

"It's a crime," the customer agreed, laughing at his own joke. Turning away, the man made his way among the crowd, holding a newspaper over his head against a new burst of rain that sent people scurrying beneath trees. Here and there posses of children ran wildly between the legs of adults, leaving chaos in their wake. Along the paths retired men sat on long benches, their faces lined and defiant. At the far end of the park, a group gathered to watch a bout of blindfolded boxing. Those spectating laughed as the two fighters swung expectantly into the air at opposite ends of the ring. Some called out advice, though each fighter mostly kept to his own instincts, lashing at the air until each looked pathetic and exhausted.

Toward evening the crowd began to disperse. Picnics were gathered, children found, and husbands retrieved. Crossing King Street, the road became clogged with people. Some walked arm in arm, singing and dancing as they manoeuvred among the line of vehicles in the street.

To Earl Pryce, however, the dancers milling about his car must have appeared as some bloody foreshadow of the Carmagnole, leading him off to La Guillotine. Earl began gesturing to a group in front of his car.

One woman tapped on the window to chastise him.

"Hey there fella, what's yer hurry?"

"Idiots," he hissed, looking out at them with revulsion. "This is almost tribal," he scoffed, losing patience.

But just as Pryce began losing his temper, another torrent of rain dropped from the sky and those standing around went looking for shelter, and the line of vehicles began to move again.

The house Earl had bought was an impressive home of Connecticut brownstone with a mammoth red maple whose branches hung protectively over the front lawn. From the number of other vehicles on the street, Earl could see he was late. Inside, he found his wife waiting at the door with a cup of tea in one hand and a newspaper in the other.

"Now, isn't this your vision of Heaven?" she asked. "No, no. The tea is mine. You'll find some inside. Perhaps one of the guests will show you where everything is."

"Sorry," he whispered. "Got caught in the demonstration over by the park."

Penny only frowned.

"I'm sorry, Pen, I am."

"It was your idea to have this little party of ours in the city."

"And aren't you glad I did? Can you imagine entertaining

all our friends up there in this rain? I'm glad we decided to have it here."

"Yes, well that may be. But how do you think I felt opening the paper this afternoon to find you had changed your mind?"

"What are you talking about? We finalized all this days ago."

"Someone forgot to tell the paper that," and she thrust it into his hands. Part way down the *In Society* section read:

> *Mr. and Mrs. Earl Pryce are entertaining*
> *guests at their country house for the*
> *evening. Friends are invited to celebrate*
> *the news of their first child.*

"You arranged the announcement."

Earl glanced at her. "It's obviously my mistake."

"I spent the afternoon setting it right."

Her husband looked apologetic. "That's my girl. Saving the day again."

Penny leaned forward, spilling some of her tea. "It's a good thing you were late. Your girl was bloody annoyed."

Slipping upstairs to the bedroom, Earl changed and re-emerged five minutes later trailing a wake of apologies and smiles.

"Honestly, I don't know how she stands me. All work and no play. Paul, Catherine, so glad you found us. I suppose you heard of my little error? Don't know what I was thinking of, probably the thrill of fatherhood. Oh thank you, Maggs, I would. A little more milk maybe. Not too black. Is that your Maxwell I saw on the street? I always thought of you as the respectable sort—not zipping around town in something fast! Don't let Pen see it, that'll be the next thing she wants. Virginia, you didn't bring your husband, did you? You know we really don't—oh, there you are old man. Your wife was just saying the most frightful things about you. Of course, we know you had to bring her, but really, Richard! You remember what a spectacle she makes of herself . . ."

And in this way he made his way among his guests, joking and charming from one end of the room to the other. Aware always of his wife's gaze, and the amusement he was providing her.

"Marcus? We never invited you! Honey, perhaps you should lock up the wine. Marcus showed up anyway."

Earl glanced at his wife, winking.

More people arrived, and food passed above the rising stratum of conversation. Two maids hired for the occasion appeared with champagne on silver trays, and the guests blushed and pretended to feel naughty.

"Yes," another woman whispered. "It's amazing how much better it tastes when it's illicit."

Someone behind her started to giggle.

"Bea, you really are drunk."

"Oh kind sir," smiling lavishly, "one should never rush a lady."

Earl laughed again, refilling her glass himself.

On his way back to the kitchen, Earl bumped into the Aldman brothers. As partners in one of Toronto's financial houses, the Aldmans had helped bankroll the expansion of Leda Steel during the War. They were what was known as high rollers, despising the miserly nature of the times and, consequently, adoring Earl Pryce.

"How are you?" Peter offered, searching in his coat for a cigar. "It's a relief to find you here."

Earl smiled, taking their coats. "Yes, I was as surprised as you."

"Obviously neither of you were hurt. That must be a consolation."

His host laughed, glancing sideways at him. "Peter, what are you talking about? If you think I'm going to waste good champagne on someone with your manners, you'd better turn back now."

Sean, the older brother, looked at him closely. "I dare say it's us that should be buying you a drink. Must be a bit shook up. When was it, by the way? You did awfully well transporting yourself here. In such order, too."

Earl struggled to keep up his smile. "Whatever are you talking about?"

Having lighted the cigar, Peter stared a moment at the match before blowing it out. "Why your house, man! You don't need to play it off with us. We were just there. Must have been quite a show!"

"My house?"

"Met your man up there. Asked where you might be, so we brought him with us."

"My man?" Earl stood completely confused, straining to seem amused.

"Tall oxen sort. Barely fit in the back," and at that the two men melted into the crowd in search of ineligible women.

It was nearly dark as Earl stepped out into the cool night. On the lawn stood Jarvis Mekes.

"You're all right, then?"

"Of course I'm all right. What's this—"

"And your wife?"

Earl was becoming frustrated. "She's serving tea at the moment. What is this about?"

Mekes looked at him gravely. "When were you last up at your house?"

"This morning. What's going on?"

Mekes was still for a moment. "Have you a car here?"

"Of course."

"Then drive me back."

"Damn it, just tell me. What the hell happened?"

"It's blown."

"What?"

"The house."

"The house?"

"Yes. It's blown."

The drive out to the country took nearly half an hour, though to Earl it seemed like twice that. The farmer would say nothing more, and so the only thing for Earl to do was to duck out of the party with as much grace as possible. Penny was understandably furious but hid it well, joking with the guests.

"Sometimes I worry there's another woman," she groaned.

Earl laughed louder than anyone as he slipped on his coat.

"Won't be long folks. Honey, watch out, Marcus is making for the liquor cabinet again."

The country lay in darkness as the car passed up the laneway, and it was a moment before he was able to make out the house in the dull glow of the head lights. The verandah was buried in a knot of lumber and slate shingles. The north wall alone remained standing with a portion of the floor boards from the second storey still hanging from their supports.

Earl parked the car, leaving the headlights on to illuminate the wreckage. Pieces of his home lay everywhere. At first Earl thought it must have been a storm or a tornado.

"An act of God . . ." he whispered stupidly.

Jarvis came up quietly beside him. "The only miracle is that you weren't in it."

Pryce was too amazed to reply.

It was like a dream: every thoughtless article of his life lay before him, now horrible and twisted as a severed limb. Paper and shards of photographs rested calmly on the lawn. From the branches of a nearby tree hung a ghostly tangle of clothes and linen, flecked with pieces of glass that gleamed like stars in the headlights.

Jarvis Mekes spoke to him in hushed tones before walking across the fields to his own home. Earl left everything, as though touching it would make it real. Even the dawn could not wash the shadow from his face.

When the sun had fully broken above the horizon, Sean Aldman drove up the lane with Penny in the front seat beside him. Earl did not notice them approach, and he was surprised to hear his wife's voice behind him.

"What—what happened here?"

He turned blankly to face her. "Mekes saw it all," he said after a moment. "Some people about the house. I guess he surprised them. A little while later the whole place blew up."

They stood like that for a long time, neither one speaking. Eventually Earl stirred, and this time he spoke without looking at his wife.

"At least someone believes what they read in the papers."

Penny looked at him, her voice growing cold. "Did you tell the police?"

Earl shook his head.

"Why not?"

Pryce shook his head resolutely. "No."

"What's going on? Why won't you tell the police? Someone destroyed our home!"

Earl's mind drifted now, farther and farther from his wife. "They're trying to kill me," he murmured.

"Who?"

"It's funny, though," again to himself. "I never thought they had the balls."

Penny stomped her foot. "Damn it, answer me! Who?"

Earl rocked silently on his heels. "Just like J. P. Morgan," he whispered, and this time he almost smiled.

The next morning Penny and Earl Pryce boarded the morning train to Detroit. Penny's hand rested uneasily on her stomach, her body rocking with the train. In the distance, behind the modest stubble of homesteads, a soft glow was settling across the scalp of fields.

When they stopped at Woodstock, Earl watched from his window as Penny met her sister on the platform. Behind him a conductor stepped back into the compartment.

"Is this the last bag, sir?"

Earl turned to look at him. "No, not that one. That is going on with me."

"You can nap if you'd like. I'll be by to wake you when we make the border."

Pryce nodded, handing the man a coin. "Be sure that you do."

∽

The two men waited almost half an hour in the ditch by the road. After scouting out the area, they ran swiftly up to the house, and Gopnik left Thomas on watch while he jimmied a side door by the kitchen. Inside, he quickly looked about the main floor before finding his way into the cellar. Taking a minute to orient himself, he decided on the south-easterly corner of the house, just below the dining room.

"This will do," he whispered to himself. "Get 'em where they'll eat."

Using twine to strap it to the joists, Gopnik packed in the dynamite a stick at a time. When it was done, he lifted up the right leg of his pants and pulled off a coil of fuse tied to his calf. He ran a long piece from each stick, then spliced each one and grafted them into a single fuse that he ran over to the southwest corner. Here he dug into his shirt for a candle with a deep groove notched at its base. Searching about in the shadows, he stuck the bottom of the candle onto a piece of nail protruding from the foundation. As he was wrapping the fuse around the groove, he heard Thomas's voice from the top of the stairs.

"Move it, someone's coming up the lane!"

Gopnik froze, too scared in that instant even to swear. He had literally spent years reinventing the moment of vengeance—how he would do it, the method of detonation— but never in this fantasy had he ever been caught. Setting the fuse, he knelt down to light a match, holding it beneath the wick until it lit.

"Get up here," Thomas hissed from the doorway.

Gopnik looked hesitantly at his work. "It'll have to do," he lamented.

In his hurry Gopnik had forgotten to support the candle properly. Though crude, the angle at which the wick sat dramatically affected the time it took to burn down. Standing upright such a candle could take four or five times as long to burn as one on a tilt. As a result, the explosion that was to go off some time during dessert took place only a hour after Gopnik had lit it.

The two men turned at the distant sound of the blast.

"So early?" Gopnik wondered aloud.

"Sounds just fine to me," Thomas replied coldly.

"You fool," he panted. "Gives us less time to get away."

They ran on in silence now, saving their breath. The shirts of both men were soaked with perspiration, and in a little while, they stopped to catch their breath at the edge of the next concession.

Thomas tried to keep his hands from shaking. He suddenly felt caught, more than poverty had ever trapped him.

"Will they call out the police?"

"You betcha," Gopnik was speaking quickly. "They'll want to search for survivors first, but it won't take long for them to come out looking. They'll have cars too. It'll take 'em a while to find our trail, but once they do, it'll be pretty quick from there. With some of the crops off we've fewer places to hide. Got maybe two hours, three if they're slow."

"Be enough?"

Gopnik looked up at the sun before nodding. "If we keep moving."

The two set out again, each man trying not to think about getting caught.

But the hunters never came. At about the time Pryce first learned of the explosion, the two men were bunking down as usual in Miss Pross's boarding house.

"Got a big day tomorrow," Gopnik yawned.

Small talk, though, was impossible for Thomas, who lay in the crowded bunk where he had slept each night since leaving home. Lying there, he scanned the dark silhouettes of those around him, while behind his eyes ran images and thoughts of what he had done, repeating themselves again and again, like a broken movie reel.

Unable to remain still, he stepped outside to smoke on the porch. It was a cloudy night, and the air tingled with the promise of rain. His hand shook as he blew out the match, spitting into the dark as he exhaled.

What am I going to do? he thought, not daring to speak out loud.

The next day he woke and ate his breakfast with the other borders, keeping his eyes on the plate before him. At the far corner of the table, Gopnik laughed loudly with those around him, chewing a piece of sausage in the side of his mouth as he talked. Thomas was not the only one to notice his friend's unusual loquacity, and some of those sitting near Thomas turned to him, amused.

"Who'd he screw?"

"I could use a piece of that."

"Get in line, fella."

"No, no. Women have always found me to their liking."

Someone snorted.

"Your mamma tell you that?"

Thomas made an effort to laugh at them. "You know, Goppy . . ." he said, before returning to his meal.

The rest of the day went like any other day, and while this brought a sense of security to Gopnik, it also made him more anxious.

"Why haven't we heard anything?" he asked out loud. "No one's said a thing all day to me. You?"

Thomas shook his head. "Nothing."

"What the hell's going on? When Cataract blew, it was the only thing they could talk about."

"Maybe it's a secret investigation," he replied, almost hopefully.

Gopnik just shook his head. Like most extremists, he was locked into the psychology of retaliation. Anything else left him suspicious, and his initial exhilaration quickly faded.

"This is no good to us at all."

A week passed and still nothing was heard.

What frightened Thomas was not discovery, but the lack of alternatives he felt. Though he would never have suspected it beforehand, his involvement with the plot to kill Earl Pryce had trapped him into trying again. The impulse to smash and ruin gripped him even while a part of him looked on in horror. Without the bandage of social reprisal, with no one demanding reciprocity, his own conscience could only bleed.

During this time, a change took place in Thomas. Something like resignation sat now, dark and heavy on his chest, and its lingering corruption could be seen in the fatalism with which he lived. At work, Thomas treated the dangers around him like annoyances to be scorned rather than feared. One day, working too close to one of the chutes, a chest-sized piece of ore spilled over the edge and landed a yard or so from where he was standing.

"Watch what you're about," the crane operator had yelled. "One of those'll break open your head!"

Thomas had only shrugged. Of course it would.

Meanwhile, Gopnik's uneasiness festered until he began looking for problems. The following week, one of his crew didn't show for work, and Gopnik flew into a rage. Throwing a shovel into his oven, he accused Gall of getting the man fired.

"Is that why Joe's not here, eh? Didn't like him did you?"

Gall looked up from his pad. "You know I can't do that. I should be asking you where the rest of your crew is. You're more likely to know than I am."

Gopnik straightened his cap. It was all quite true.

Gall shook his head, but paused before turning. "That shovel is coming out of your pay, by the way."

Gopnik only looked at him.

Gall wrote something down on his pad and moved off.

Earl Pryce returned alone from Windsor the Sunday after the explosion. The following Tuesday, a train pulled into Hamilton station slightly ahead of schedule. Among those to get off were four men, each wearing dark, unassuming suits. One of the men waited by the luggage car, holding several of the red claim tickets used by the Grand Trunk line. The oldest of the four walked casually into the station. When he re-emerged, he nodded to the other three who followed him out to a waiting taxi.

They were dropped off in front of the Royal Hotel on James Street at the corner of Merrick. Again, the older of the four went into the building alone, and when he returned the others followed him through the wide lobby to their rooms. That day, the older man went out in the afternoon for almost an hour while the others remained inside the hotel.

The following night, however, after finishing their meals, each of them left the hotel alone. The last to leave was the older

man. He ate slowly, as though contemplating his food's digestion. It was warm in the hotel restaurant. A single bead of
sweat appeared over his left temple and the man reached into
his jacket, pushing aside a blue fold of paper for a handkerchief
that he used to wipe his forehead. The bill came and he asked
the waiter to call him a taxi.

That night, Joseph Moylan stepped out of the narrow two-
storey walk-up he shared with his wife and youngest son. It
was warm for being almost October, he thought, and left his
coat open to let the evening breeze brush against his chest. And
so it was that Joe was not paying much attention when a figure
appeared behind him and something hard came down across
his shoulders. He fell like a stone, and it was almost a minute
before he knew what was going on.

When he came to, he was in complete darkness and unable
to move his arms. "What the . . ."

From the darkness, something struck the side of his head
and a wad of cloth was forced into his mouth. At the same
moment someone lighted a match in front of his face and he
immediately stilled, his eyes dilating frantically at the light. A
candle was placed on the ground between his legs. Looking
down at himself, Joe saw that he was naked. His breathing
grew hard and quick as he searched the darkness.

Beside him came a voice against his ear.

"Hello, Joseph. No, don't try to look at me; we might have
to hit you again. You seem a little frightened by all this, but if
you're helpful, I promise it will all be over soon enough. That's
right, Joe; I've come for your help. I do hope you can help
me . . . I only want to go home like you, to have a cup of tea
with my wife. But if you don't seem helpful, well, then it might
go badly. I might have to ask my friend here to cut your balls

off and put one in each of your pockets to take back to your wife. You believe me, don't you, Joseph? I don't have to take just one, do I, to let you know I'm an honest man? No, I can see you believe me. Good. You know why I'm here, don't you, Joe? Sure you do. I can see you're a smart fella. I like that, I really do. The dumb ones are so eager to bleed. I just knew you'd be able to help me. You see, someone's hurt a friend of mine, Joe. And I'd like to talk with whoever did that. It wasn't you, was it? You're sure? You see how much my friend likes his knife, don't you? No. Forgive me, Joe. I do not believe you did this thing to my friend."

The lips were hot against Joe's ear now.

"But I think you might know . . . I think you might know who I'm looking for. Yes, I'm sure of it. I'm sure you are going to help me, aren't you, Joe? You don't want your son to see you this way do you? That big fella down there sticking from your mouth? Smile on your face. They'd all call you a faggot Joe. Your boy thinking his father was a cocksucking faggot. I bet they wouldn't even bury you in the church! They're heartless bastards in the church you know . . . So what's it gonna be? You gonna help me? I didn't want to rush you. Just let you know where the land lies. Now I'm going to reach around and take your underwear out of your mouth and you know what I want to hear, Joe. You know what I'm expecting you to say. You're not going to disappoint me, are you? No, no, you're not. Thank you. I can't tell you how happy you've made me . . ."

When it had happened, when he had broken, they left him there to untie himself, to find his pants in the dark emptiness of his neighbour's shed. But before going home, Joe drew himself into a ball and wept bitterly on the floor of cold and indifferent earth.

Storm clouds, so ubiquitous in October, lurked across the top of the city like a plague, staining the streets with seeds of black water. The mills and factories began releasing hundreds of men back into the city. Over their heads smokestacks, poking from the harbour shore like the teeth of a broken comb, seemed to feed the stratum of cloud. But as the sun rose over the lake, an unguent of orange light coated the earth, and the bleeding clouds were slowly eclipsed by dawn.

Mary Oban now took in laundry from those living in the larger homes south of Main Street, and in the evenings she and Mona went late to the moviehouse downtown where they cleaned the floors and washrooms. Hal had moved out a month earlier to take a job in Toronto, which left Gabe alone to look after the house and meals. He was not uncomfortable with these household chores, but instead found an odd pride in the work. He had grown stronger in the past four years, and though he was slight for nineteen, the child was gone from his face. In its place had settled the appearance of a man and though it fit him like an uncle's suit, it brought a shy sort of confidence.

The same, however, could not be said of Mona. For almost two weeks after losing her baby she lay in bed with a fever, while Mary sat with her, speaking in a voice even Gabe had never known. After the fever left, Mona remained in her room.

It annoyed him, and he had spoken about it to his mother, knowing what she thought of idleness.

"What do you know about this?" she'd shot at him.

Gabe had said nothing more after that, and returned to bringing Mona her meals with grudging obedience. It would not be until much later, when he had met the woman he would marry, that Gabriel understood how hard he had been.

When she grew stronger, Mona came down in the morning and ate with them. But instead of the bright dresses she had always worn, Mona wore some of Mary's older things, pinning a leaf-coloured shawl about herself. She spoke quietly now, no longer challenging Mary or the workings of the house. No impulse for autonomy or rebellion remained, only the quiet inertia of the bleeding.

In this way, their lives came together each day to eke out an existence, defending the rude sanctity of their home.

"Work keeps a soul in line," Mary often asserted over breakfast. "If it weren't for it there would be no living with yourself."

These words always made Gabe smile into his porridge, and he would remember how as a child he had thought his body must be a miserable place for his soul.

One morning after the copper coal bin by the stove had been filled, Gabe left with the wagon while his mother and Mona began heating water for that day's washing. Approaching the market, he felt the slow rhythms of home knocked from his shoulders by the rough energy of the crowd—babushkas squawking over loaves of Portuguese bread; the unshaven men behind the stalls with closely-cropped hair and cigarettes cocked behind their ears; brown-handed farm women wreathed in auras at once curious and repulsive; baskets of pigeons and rabbits looking on with igno-rant terror; and most of all, the sound of his own voice lost in the city's ear.

Among the fruit sellers, Gabe found Mahonia sitting beside one of the stalls.

"Gabe!" he yelled, coming over to pat the boy's face. "Lambro was just asking when you're coming to work for him, huh? I've told him what a gardener you are. Come over and say hello. Lambro, here's the boy."

Gabe smiled. Mahonia's friend brought out the softer side of his temperament.

"Gabe, Gabe, Gabe. I have just the job. You mustn't say no. My boss, he's looking for pickers . . . easiest work in the world. None of this bending over in the dirt like my friend here. No. But standing in the sun among the vines." He put an arm around the boy's shoulders, so full of faith in the body. "It's beautiful work. Both my sons are at it. I cannot understand why it's so hard to find good people. Soldiers—they're not interested. Can't meet women, they say. Bah! Not true. Too interested in working at some big factory and making lots of money and never letting the sun on their faces. No, don't shake your head at me! Only think about it, that's all I'm saying. Work won't start till summer—you have lots of time."

Mahonia laughed. "Ask him what he's doing with all them grapes."

Lambro grinned and cocked his head instead of blushing. "What are you saying to me? You accusing me of . . . of what?" He winked at Gabe. "No temperance people bother with my wares," he exclaimed. "Wine is as legal as water," and here he paused to tap his jaw with one finger.

Mahonia laughed again.

Gabe only smiled.

In a little while he moved on toward the butcher's in search of sausage and perhaps a chop, if he could find something cheap. It began to rain again, though gently, and Gabe pulled the rim of his cap about his ears.

"Hey there."

Looking up he almost didn't recognize the man, his face had so altered.

"Hello Gabe."

He stopped casually, as if interested in the price of apples.

"You're not at work."

An indifferent shrug. "Just got off."

"They put you on the night shift?"

"I asked for a change. It's what I got."

"Oh," the boy looked again at his father. "It's just you; you hate nights."

A flash of anger behind the eyes, extinguishing in a sigh. "You get used to it."

Thomas became quiet and turned to stare at the faces pushing about him, and his voice suddenly grew pained. "How is . . . everyone is alright?"

"We're alright."

"Good. Why you shopping today?"

Gabe forgot himself and grinned. "It's my job while mother and . . . while they get to the washing."

Thomas smiled and shook his head, the bitterness almost disappearing. "She was ever one to clean up after others."

Gabe looked among the apples for something to say. "You getting on?"

He tried to grin. "I'm okay."

A man pushed between them with a crate of lettuce.

A long moment passed, silent and understood. The boy shuffled his shoe against the pavement. The clouds began to blur into mud and water.

"Well. I oughta . . ." And as he pushed past, the boy felt the man's fingers brush against his wrist.

"Shall I say hi for you?"

Thomas turned, squinting at his son with a sudden gleam of optimism. "Sure. Why don't you do that," and he smiled.

Gabe watched his father taper into the crowd. There was no moral victory, no justice in his father's suffering. Only a mutual misery. The blood of Mona's dead child hung everywhere, splashed over every door post. On the way home he passed a wall on which someone had written about the Communists. It seemed almost sexual to him. That quick passionate moment in the dark, the scattering of red paint along the pavement:

PRAVDA!

Such an elusive word, seduced into the pantries of under-fed zealots, forced to kneel before the penny icons of third-rate gods. The politician's beautiful whore.

The truth. The truth, you knew, was like sugar: sweet—the way it melted the knot you kept in your chest for those you loved—but bad for you too. So you only indulged in it now and then, one grain at a time. Rehearsing it from silent lips at night where it couldn't damage the stained glass of deception, screaming it instead into your pillow where it could lie among the plucked feathers.

That evening over dinner he mentioned meeting his father. There had been little response at first, and he had waited for his mother's reaction while she spooned food onto their plates.

"He sounds as if he's happier where he is," she said, looking at her son.

Gabe began to sweat, a panicked sensation growing in his bowels. A spasm of familial blackmail.

"Yes," he muttered. "He seemed happy."

Mona looked up from her sausage, crying quietly the way women knew how. His mother didn't even scowl.

They looked at each other over their plates, their thoughts rattling about in the sugar bowl.

§

Gopnik had grown deeply sullen since the bombing. When the office of Cataract had been destroyed everyone had known, newspapers taking the news all over the province. But now, after destroying the very home of a mill owner, not a word had been spoken of it. And the silence had begun to eat at him.

After fighting with Gall, he had put in for a transfer and gotten the night shift. It had been an easy transition. It was always difficult getting men to work nights, and two weeks later Thomas had followed him. The move had done little good for Gopnik and he rarely slept now, harassed by the sterility of his crime.

Thomas found Gopnik waiting for him on the porch of the boarding house, smoking one cigarette after another.

"Whatcha doing?"

Gopnik wouldn't look at him, but kept his stare focussed on the cigarette between his fingers. "There's bin trouble."

"What's that mean?"

He suddenly threw away the cigarette, slipping on his hat as he stood up.

"C'mon, I'll show you."

"Where we going?"

"I said, I'll show you."

"But we'll miss dinner!"

"Don't worry about your appetite," he muttered. "Just come on. You'll see."

Suddenly a calmness came over Thomas and he immediately forgot about his son. *At last* was all he could think. It was happening.

Thomas almost had to run to keep up with Gopnik as they traced a series of alleys and back lanes to the row of shops where they had left the Party meeting four months earlier. There was no back door; instead the two caught at a fire escape and pulled themselves up to a window that opened quite suddenly as they approached.

"I told them I'd bring you back with me," Gopnik explained.

The room was almost in complete darkness and each man stood for a moment while their eyes adjusted.

They were met by a woman.

"You're back," she said dully, as a matter of fact.

A figure on the bed broke into loud coughing.

"John?"

"She said you had been here."

"I've come back with a friend."

Even in the light Thomas could not place the man's voice with his face, which was swollen and bruised beyond recognition. Pushing them aside the woman began dabbing at her husband's face with a wet cloth.

"You should be quiet," she whispered.

"Soon," he said, reaching up for her hand. "I have to talk with them first."

"Later, they can wait until . . ."

"Please. Only a minute," his voice pleading. "Check on the child. This is important."

There was a long moment as she looked at him.

"I'll be back in a minute."

When she had gone, Gopnik stepped forward, leaning over the man as if looking for him among the wreckage of the face.

"Is there anything I can get you?"

The head moved a little. "No time."

"Who did this to you?"

"They found out—they found out about the Party."

"Who?"

"Too many of them. I tried to run but . . ."

"Who?" Gopnik hissed. "You must tell me who."

"Don't know, but they asked why I did it; I didn't know and so they kept hitting me. He wouldn't believe me," and now when he spoke his voice broke. "He read my name from a list, said my friends had given it to him. Said I'd been betrayed; I had no one . . ."

Gopnik felt the bed begin to shake.

"What did you tell him?" Thomas whispered, scared now for the first time since the explosion. "Did you tell him about the rest of us?"

The man began to weep. "It didn't matter. I saw the list in his hand."

Forgetting himself, Gopnik grabbed the man's arm.

"List? Whose list, dammit? I can't fight back if you don't tell me!"

John wailed, as if recalling a nightmare. "Can't anyone hear me? I don't know!"

At this, Thomas loosened Gopnik's grip. "Alright John, you done well by telling us. You've shown thought for your common man despite differences between us. We'll spread the word to the others and let 'em know. No need for anyone else to get involved."

John shook his head again, frustrated. "You don't understand—the list."

"What of it?"

"You were both on it."

Some said it had been Thomas's idea. Perhaps they suspected he understood more of his boss than he would admit, not letting himself know out loud, but keeping it hidden like a dagger inside some sleeve of memory. Knowing that he had—more than Gopnik would ever understand—the secret to hurt a man deeply, with obscene simplicity. Knew the point of breaking because he had felt that same axis in himself give way and collapse.

Pain is like that. It can find its twin in anyone.

It was more than daring, Gopnik had to admit. And there would be no going back, not this time. He had been surprised at the extravagance of Thomas's proposal, surprised the way a wolf is the first time its pup finds the jugular.

As a crime, it could not go unnoticed. It would demand reaction. There would be outrage and accusations, upheaval, suffering. It would bring fire—a fire they must trust others to fan.

Gopnik nearly shuddered with anticipation to think of it.

Thomas also knew that he would have to leave everything as soon as it was done. Yet the moment he spoke of it to Gopnik, it had brought a frantic sense of courage, a kind of redemption from the pitying contempt he had seen in his son's eyes that day at the market. It was strange that the prospect of becoming a fugitive brought to him a feeling of tangibility, an emotional steadfastness that he had almost forgotten. And as the words slipped from his lips, he felt the irrational sense of hope found only among the drowning.

Thomas suffered a small grin as he turned to Gopnik. "The ovens. We'll blow up the ovens."

The two men listened to the deafening sound of rain against the corrugated roof above them, where the shadows hung in the rafters like buzzards. They chose to act on a Sunday, perhaps because they knew there would be almost no one working and plenty of time to do what they came for.

Making sure no one was about, the two men crossed the yard, ducking behind a row of ingots and into the mammoth furnace room. Inside they stuck close to the near wall to avoid the glow of fire which flashed across the floor. As they passed beneath the large crane, Gopnik separated from Thomas who began running the fuse through several sticks of dynamite hidden in his coat.

Climbing a ladder to the top of the crane, Gopnik began inching his way across the steel ballast. About the midway point, he paused to swing one leg over the wide beam which supported the crane's extension across the mill floor. Straddling the beam, he waved an okay at Thomas before untying the explosives from his waist.

But his arm halted in mid-wave. What he saw almost sent him crashing to floor below.

Thomas had not heard them approach, and the only warning he had was when one of them knocked the detonation caps from his hands. Something came down across his head, and had he not jumped it might have killed him there and then. For a moment he was barely aware of what was happening until someone began kicking him. Instinctively, his body tried to double up, but they were holding his ankles and he could only reach out vainly to ward off the next one, and the next, and the next.

It seemed a long time before it stopped, though for several minutes the agony had barely let him register the succession of blows. He became aware of feet walking in and out of his vision, and he tried to get up. Someone laughed and a hand slipped under his head for him to see.

Coming into focus, Thomas's eyes suddenly dilated. Across the tortured film of his gaze reflected the face of Earl Pryce, outlined in the ovens' glow.

There was a groan as Thomas tried to move again, and he felt hands tearing at his clothes for the rest of the dynamite. As they lifted him the touch of someone's face drew close to his, bringing a delicate hiss.

"This is *my* revenge . . ."

The voice sounded soft to Thomas, like something said in church. It was followed by movement, and another voice somewhere more distant. And then the savage, rushing, familiar mouth of fire.

five

Hannah Barrett met and married Calvin Creighton, a man ten years her senior, in Greece where she was travelling with her family. Calvin was there as a pilgrim of sorts, having quit school five years earlier to see the land of the only story that ever interested him. The year was 1897. They met among the skeletal columns at Delphi, she on a tour with her father, he alone. In a coincidental turn, Calvin and his future father-in-law struck up a discussion on some point of Classical architecture. In the process, they discovered themselves to be fellow countrymen, and the younger of the two was promptly invited to dinner. That night, they talked long after the women had gone to bed, each sharing with the other a mutual affection for Homer, travel, and brandy, though not entirely in that order. Greece was, for both men, a paradise, and over the next month a sort of boozy fraternity formed between them.

During these visits Calvin began to take notice of Hannah Barrett.

Hannah's beauty had always been one of disinterest, a fact that made her all the more extraordinary in an era of anxious contrivance. Next to her mother she wore comparatively little makeup or jewellery. Her lack of adornment heightened the impression she had on men, though it brought her no little amount of scorn from the women who knew her. As she aged, Hannah allowed her face and body to do so as well. Though she continued to dress respectably, she resisted the enamel of creams and paints normally associated with fading youth.

By the time Calvin met her Hannah had, as they say, grown into herself, though she remained shy with new people. After the second week of his visits, however, she began feeling more at ease around this blunt and strident man who tried to catch her eye across the dinner table. Paul Barrett also noticed his protégé's growing affection, and encouraged it with uncharacteristic subtlety.

During this time the tensions growing in Thessaly finally came to a head, and Greece went to war with Turkey. The consequent atmosphere of heroism spread to more than one tourist, and Calvin decided to embrace the mood by offering his hand to Hannah before she evacuated. Surprising herself as much as anyone around her, Hannah accepted. It is unclear whether Calvin really expected her to suffer his offer. Some have suggested he was looking for an excuse to abandon reason and join the Greeks' fight. Like any hero he had ever read about, Calvin was waiting for a woman to drive him upon the stake of fate. The problem was she accepted him, and as a result he was forever kept back from his moment of glory.

Nonetheless, Calvin lived up to his offer and married Hannah the evening before they sailed back to Canada. It was on the boat that Hannah first felt a distance between her and her new husband. As the boat separated from the dock, she could see in his eyes that a part of him would remain there.

That night Hannah stared past his slowly rocking shoulder, searching the ceiling of their cabin for stars. Above the cadence of their breathing she heard the soft moan of the boat, and the nocturnal pulse of waves. The following morning, she walked about deck before going in to breakfast. Hannah found her husband already seated and eating.

"Darling," he greeted her. "You slept well?"

She nodded, looking about for a waiter. "You've already ordered?"

"Yes," looking over his coffee cup. "I thought you might be awhile and I was famished. You seemed a little scattered this morning."

Hannah flushed.

Calvin looked down at his napkin. "Shall I order?"

"Please."

He waved at a passing waiter.

"Tell your cook in there that this was a wonderful breakfast!"

"Of course."

"And when you have a chance, would you bring me out another plate of eggs?"

"And for the lady?"

Hannah looked up meekly. "Toast."

"Is that all?"

In a short while, the waiter reappeared, carrying two plates. Calvin lunged over his meal.

"You're not hungry at all, are you?"

Hannah watched as he wiped up the yellow mess with a corner of bread.

"You certain you don't want something more?"

She shuddered suddenly, bending over to vomit between her feet.

It was immensely embarrassing to Hannah, though the crew was very good about it. The captain even sent her flowers, and invited her to dine at his table when she was well.

Calvin, however, had been deeply troubled by the scene, and insisted she eat in their cabin for the rest of the voyage.

"There, there," he said. "This way we'll have no more scenes."

Hannah gave birth eight months after they returned to Canada. She was very possessive of her unborn child, almost as much as her husband, and the polarization of their affection for the baby became the first seed of tension in the marriage. In the nights that followed, Calvin would get up to watch Hannah nurse their child. It was his son, he knew, yet he could see there was nothing for him to do but watch. Now and then his wife would look up at him over the child's head and smile.

"It's all right, dear," she would whisper. "You can go back to sleep."

In bed Calvin would draw the covers about himself, trying to reclaim their fleeting warmth.

As the years passed more children followed, and each woke to the world understanding themselves to be rocks on which their parents broke themselves.

&

Calvin Creighton was dying.

And like so many he went screaming too loud for anyone to hear.

With the conflict in Europe now over, a despair seemed to settle on the man just as the rest of the nation was disbanding the apparatus of war in one collective sigh. Armbands, those ebony reminders of suffering, were soon put away in boxes and attics with other artifacts of memory. Within a year, sugar and gasoline were found in plenty again. In cities and towns, church bells could be heard far out into the surrounding farms and forests, mingling the anthems of death and life.

During this time, Calvin indulged in what was still an illegal way to express self-loathing. In 1919, Calvin had gone to the polls cursing "that damned Hearst," furious that no party had the decency to look even damp, let alone wet. To show his contempt, Calvin later bragged he had written Leacock's name on the ballot and voted for him instead.

In the years that followed the War, Calvin sank resolutely into despair. Yet this despondency made no sense to those who knew him. By this time, Eddie had successfully taken over his business; he had seen both his older daughters married, and was already a grandfather. Death should have been the furthest thing from his mind. But of course it was not. Like a dog eating grass, he now drank as though hoping to vomit, as if straining to expel something corrupt within him.

Albra had survived adolescence, growing into herself in a withdrawn yet confident manner. Increasingly reclusive, she was now wholly dedicated to painting. Feeling restless and confined in her mother's front parlour, she and Arthur had gone in search of new subjects to paint. Hannah had protested at first, but her ambivalence toward her youngest child had long since silenced her anxiety over social mores, and her resistance had quickly faded.

"Fine," she had snapped. "Go if you want. It's too late now to disgrace your sisters. We'll tell the neighbours he's an uncle."

And so Albra was freed—for the first time in her life—to step out of her father's home alone. She was often seen tramping about the city with her case of paints jutting from under her arm. Meeting Arthur in parks, they would continue her lessons where Albra could sit and draw the world around her. Sometimes when the work was going well, she would talk to Arthur over the top of her pad.

"It's nice here."

"Yes, it is."

"It's good to be away from things."

"I like the park," he agreed.

Her pencil paused. "Better than your teaching?"

"Better than being inside."

"Oh."

"Someday I'll take you into the country to paint."

"Peaceful?"

"Like paradise."

In a little while, he put aside his pad and looked up to see what she was doing.

"What are you sketching?"

"That fellow over there."

"The old one?"

"No, by the fountain."

Albra turned slightly so he could see over her shoulder. Beside the path a man was drinking from a tap; when he straightened, he saw they were looking at him.

Arthur waved.

The man stood motionless for an instant before nodding. His sleeves hung limp at his sides.

Arthur sighed quietly, his voice suddenly hushed.

"Oh."

"Yes," she said. "There are a lot of them."

He turned back to his sketching, and for the next hour they worked in silence.

Feeling her legs growing stiff, Albra finally stood and stretched with satisfaction.

"It's late," she observed.

It was May and there were plenty of people about enjoying the afternoon sun. Albra walked slowly so that Arthur could look at the crowd. When they came to the corner, he squinted into the street in search of a trolley, talking as they waited.

"I saw a drunk man the other day," he said. "A soldier, I think. He had some frightening metal contraption about his head. He wasn't begging, but I found myself feeling ashamed that I couldn't help him . . ."

He caught at her sleeve as she went to step onto the trolley. He smiled apologetically at her, as if recalling something sad.

Letting two women step on ahead of her, Albra paused to look at him.

"You make it out to be worse than it is," she said quietly. "Sometimes I envy them."

When it rained or grew too cold to work in the park, Albra often met Arthur in his loft where they painted from the sketches they had made in better weather. Sometimes his wife Evelyn would visit with their child, carrying a box of sandwiches and the boiled eggs which Arthur loved. Evelyn had quickly won Albra over, disarming the girl with her confidence. On entering the loft, Evelyn would hand the child to Arthur so that she might look over their work.

"Be careful not to copy him too closely," she advised. "That's always the danger in a tutor."

Albra could only smile. "I'll make sure to give him credit when I'm famous."

Evelyn turned thoughtfully on the crate where she was sitting.

"Do you think you're ready to show it?"

"Show?"

"Yes."

"What do you mean?"

Evelyn scowled. "What do you plan to do with your painting?"

"Like what?"

"Perhaps you could sell a piece? Make some money for yourself."

Albra looked stunned.

The baby gurgled to herself.

"It hadn't occurred to me," she explained.

When her work went poorly, Albra sometimes went outside for a walk, leaving the two alone while she looked about the narrow streets in hope of inspiration. On these trips, she met some of the other artists who shared the house. Among them, she discovered a handful of people who were willing to take her seriously.

Sitting in a chair or on an upturned box, she would sip the bitter coffee one of the men shared with her and listen while they talked of a world she had hardly glimpsed. They were impassioned conversations mostly, strewn with notions and words one never heard in polite company.

"If I learned anything in France," one man began, "it's to distrust sentiment."

Somewhere in the house a door slammed.

"You can't do that," another protested. "It's not human. What you call sentiment, I would call love. And love is not a luxury, but a demand. It's forced on one by a need for purpose in existence, an anchor in the tide towards annihilation. Our souls crave meaning. Why else would they cling to the sordid impulses of our bodies?"

Someone made a rude joke which Albra did not understand.

From the corner, a slim fellow with greying hair passed around slices of overripe apple. Some of the men dangled cigarettes between their fingers, blowing the blue smoke through their noses.

Arthur sat sharpening pencils with a pocket knife, his brow knitted with thought. "I agree with you. Emotions bridge the chasm between flesh and soul. But you can't resign it to nature, unless you're a Darwinist or something. It's up to the individual to be courageous enough to release their grasp on reason."

"No more of your blessed philosophy, please."

"Speaking of the irrational," piped a tired-looking man with bad teeth. "You're dreaming if you think anyone with power would give up the love affair with Voltaire and reason. How do you think one gets to parliament in the first place!"

"Do you know any reasonable politicians?"

"Don't kid yourself. They're all that way."

"You're being too simplistic again. Each of us has influence. Until the charwoman frees her mind, we cannot expect a prime minister to do it."

"Here we go . . ."

Some shook their heads. "The People first and all that, you mean?"

"I'll take it over your morals!"

"At least I have some."

"If only your church did, too."

A foot shuffled.

"Easy," someone muttered.

"I don't see any point in placing my trust upon a species that has done nothing but try to destroy itself. Why should I have faith in something so imperfect? So morally insane? Surely there is a higher order? One that keeps us from smashing ourselves—the way you keep your child there from tumbling down stairs. If there wasn't, we'd have all been dead long ago."

"You might consider that such a catastrophe is a wholly reasonable fate for humanity. Perhaps it is natural that we extinguish ourselves. Your theory is fixated on the notion that we are meant to survive as a species, that we will perpetuate ourselves indefinitely. Even with a cursory understanding of history, one would conclude that what you say is wrong. If I were religious I would say God wants us all dead."

The man with bad teeth spread a piece of newspaper across his lap to collect crumbs.

"No. There is only one God, and that is the self. If God were to want us dead, it is He who would be committing suicide. I can't believe in that. The prime impulse of the human spirit is to survive—to survive through expression. To create. At their core all forms of creation are expressions of identity."

"This smacks of vanity to me," another disagreed. "Why should you or I or that child there count for a hill of beans? Didn't the War prove that? A bullet is the epitome of fate: oblivious and lethal. Our only value is in our numbers. If our mothers had had fewer of us, we might all be speaking German now. As it turns out, they did not, and so the whole world will speak English."

Someone passed Albra another mug of coffee.

"How is it, then, that as individuals we can be at the same time infinitely the same and infinitely different? How can you dismiss identity with all its accompanying anxieties? If there is a God, He must be found in identity. There is no other way; there is nothing else a person can really comprehend."

"Listen to Saint Paul over here."

"Well it makes more sense than following the Russians!"

"I can think of worse paths to lead a nation down."

"Buying off the poor with bread as you go?"

"Have you met a god that didn't?"

Evelyn shook her head, rocking the child quietly on her arm. "It's all the same. One Party versus One God . . . what's the difference? If you're going to all the trouble of staging a revolution, at least you might try and be original. Why not make God a woman?"

Someone behind Albra laughed.

Arthur grinned wryly. "That would be original."

"After all, the first thing we know is a woman."

"I think motherhood has gone to your head."

"And perhaps the gin has gone to yours."

Several of the men laughed, though stiffly this time.

"A woman can be a queen, can she not? Didn't Victoria show us this?"

"The Queen's day is done."

"A sad thing too. Especially for you men. A man could live much longer under a queen in the last century than he has so far with a king in this one."

The man with bad teeth frowned and stopped chewing, swallowing what was left in his mouth.

"I'm not particular myself, one way or the other. In the end, our hunger is the cushion of every throne. We should all remember that."

&

With the loss of Thomas' wage, the meagre income they were able to gather by taking in laundry was not enough to support them in a house. Within three months, they had moved to an apartment, selling all but a few pieces of furniture. Each morning, Gabe would go about the city gathering and returning the laundry that supported their humble existence, while in the afternoons he ironed as Mona and his mother washed the clothes he had collected. It was dull work and he was easily irritated as the heat from the iron swelled the tiny flat. To escape this suffocating atmosphere, Gabe began walking in the evening down by the mills with the faint hope of seeing his father. He often thought of their last meeting in the market.

Now, behind the loading yards he watched groups of men talking with themselves. They looked up at him as he passed, and their eyes seemed to deflect his stare. Gabe could sometimes see from the street into the oven rooms, and he would wonder where his father had gone.

Occasionally, Gabe went to visit Mahonia. During one of their talks the boy was persuaded to take the job that his friend Lambro had mentioned the year before, though at first it was difficult for Gabe to accept the notion of leaving.

"No. I couldn't abandon them."

"It's only for the summer!"

Robert Bell

"Still. Who'd pick up the laundry?"

"They'd need to do less of it with you earning money out of the home. You'd be helping more this way."

"There's no saying I'd get the job."

"Of course you'll get it. Lambro will put in a word for you and it will all be settled."

Gabe was quiet for a long time, uncertain of what he was feeling.

"I'll ask my mother," he said doubtfully.

Mary surprised her son by supporting the idea right away, and her enthusiasm left him feeling offended.

For Mary, Gabe's departure brought a sense of guilty relief. Though she disliked ruminating over it, the absence of her husband had somehow soured her warmth for the boy, and Mary now found herself growing indignant with the burden of his strenuous affection. That winter, for the first time in her life, Mary came to fear weakness in herself, and to despise it utterly in men.

Exempted from temperance legislation, the vineyards of Ontario's Niagara region had prospered during the War. Each summer, an unassuming carnival of men and women were hired to tend and harvest the burgeoning crop. Among those who went to work in the summer of 1920 was Gabriel Oban, who left the city to join the seasonal migration of workers who filtered into the country.

It was not a large vineyard where he worked, consisting of twenty or so acres running along three gently-sloping hills. They were flanked by an orchard that hid a cluster of bunkies and storage sheds. Part-way up the opposite slope were three barns where the presses and barrels were stored. Behind the barns sat a house made from fieldstone where the vintner and his family lived. In May, wind carried the orchard's blossoms into the valley, covering the slopes with petals of white and pink until each vine stood like a bride at spring's altar.

Normally, the farm employed about seven people year round, though as the harvest approached, that number might increase fivefold. Through the winter, as the fields lay buried beneath drifts of snow, the valley echoed with the building of casks for the summer's wine.

The vineyard was different from anything Gabe had ever known. When he arrived, Lambro showed him to one of the bunkhouses. It was a long, one-roomed building fitted with ten beds made from pine boards and straw-filled mattresses. It was late in the day and when he had stowed his bag, Lambro walked him back out to the yard.

"Over there's the bath, and behind's the outhouses. No sense in going out now." Lambro paused and pointed up at the sun. "They'll be back any time now. Might as well come and help with dinner."

Following him across the yard of baked clay, Gabe stepped under a large tent. It had been a hot day, and the thick canvas hung limply in the sun. Just outside the tent was an open hearth with a black cauldron and Lambro sent Gabe in search of fuel to stoke the fire. He found wood stacked behind one of the bunkies. Gathering as much as he could carry, he walked back to the tent and left it beside the pot. On his second trip, Gabe had to pause and wipe the sweat from his face. Across the small stretch of grass between the bunkies were several lines for drying clothes. Seeing them made him think of his mother, and he frowned with a sudden weight in his chest. The edge of the orchard seemed to stretch out before him, each branch already bowed with the pregnant sway of fruit. From the trees and grass came the indolent drone of insects. The laundry hung heavy and still.

Gabe sighed quietly without hearing himself.

That evening, he ate with the other workers, listening as they talked. Some told of their work in the young vineyards of British Columbia and California, drawing meaningfully from their pipes as they spoke. One of the men sat sewing a hole in his trousers, his bare legs stretched out into the circle of people. Somewhere a mother was singing to her baby and across the yard children played. The man beside him passed Gabe a saucer of wine, and he sat there in the dust and gravel of the yard letting the warm feeling of the soil seep into his blood. When he closed his eyes, two of the women looked at each other and smiled, winking in the setting light.

In the morning, they rose early to a bell that rang up the hill and through the orchard from one of the pressing barns. At breakfast, they had black coffee with porridge and bread, and by sunrise Gabe found himself working among the rows of vines. There had been a drought that month and as the harvest approached it became imperative to water the vines.

"Water," explained one woman, "is the blood of the soil."

And so as the first light crept over the horizon, a staggered line could be discerned in the grey light, each person shouldering a yoke with two buckets from the creek.

At noon, Cook and her husband came around with loaves of bread and a great sphere of cheese that she carried beneath one arm. When they had done eating, the foreman sent Gabe and several others to prune while the rest continued watering.

Moving from stand to stand, a woman showed him which leaves to remove. Now and then they came upon a cluster of grapes infected with rot or insects. They were cut away from the rest and dropped to the ground where they were crushed underfoot. Looking down, Gabe watched as the juice pushed out between his sole and the earth, sinking into the cracked dirt. Once he nearly stepped onto the body of a raccoon that lay, feet in the air, beside one of the stands. Gabe pointed it out to the man working in the next row.

The man only nodded. "Poison got him," he grunted, and yelled down the slope.

In a little while, a tall fellow sauntered up, sticking the

animal on the end of a pitch fork before carrying it back down the hill.

The light grew orange and then red as dusk settled over the valley. They stopped late in the day, ambling in ones and twos toward the kitchen tent. In much this way the first two weeks passed, with Gabe growing slowly stronger and more accustomed to his work.

∽

Looking back, Albra would see that her father had begun to deteriorate long before the end. Once remote and controlled, Calvin now burst into rages at his family without provocation. Blunted accusations occurred over meals, muffled outbursts behind doors, and general disquiet. These skirmishes usually concluded with a reconciliation of sorts, but in time the conflicts always returned. Now, like a ghost, his voice carried uneasily through the large house, and his wife was glad the oldest children were no longer there to see his decline. In this way, Albra and her mother were thrust unwillingly into a confederate sympathy. They pulled closer for warmth, unconscious of the tie that bound each to a person she could never quite bring herself to like.

One afternoon, Albra returned home to a loud moaning coming from the back of the house. Opening the washroom door, she found her father lying on the tiled floor in a smear of his own excrement. Before she could get help, Calvin had made his daughter clean him.

"You can bloody well give up your artistic airs for a moment and help me!"

Albra choked back the bile forming in her mouth. A coldness came over her as she cleaned the man's grey flesh and it was only later, after help arrived, that she allowed herself the luxury of bathing.

Julius stayed well into the evening, giving Albra instructions on what to do before he left. When he had gone, she busied herself with straightening the room and speaking to her father in whispers. Not long after there was a knock at the door, and as it opened, Hannah stepped hesitantly into the bedroom.

"How is he?" she whispered.

When he saw her, the prone man abruptly gasped and grew pale.

His wife nearly shrieked. "Is he having a spell?"

As if in reply, Calvin sat up in bed and pointed at his wife. "It was you!" Then, just as abruptly, he fell back into the bed and groaned, his face withering.

Albra ushered her mother out of the room. "It's all right," she whispered. "He doesn't know what he's saying."

Hannah didn't seem to hear. "What does he mean?" she asked, staring at her daughter. "What is he accusing me of?"

When she had quieted her father, Albra went downstairs to see her mother.

Hannah was leaning against a chair in the front hall. Seeing her daughter, she straightened somewhat and tried to smile. She turned feebly toward the parlour but stopped as she reached the doorway.

"Everything has become strange, hasn't it?"

Albra sighed, her legs suddenly tired beneath her.

"What do you mean?"

Hannah blinked at her daughter as though trying to express it, this confusion she felt.

"There are periods where life seems to pause and shed the useless things from itself. There is a lull in all the activity, and everything becomes fragile. People I know die or suffer some calamity. Children get jobs and families. Others disappear into a map, rootless and vagrant. While in the corner I wait and watch, wondering what will happen to me . . ."

Occasionally, Albra took the trolley across the city to where Arthur and Evelyn lived. There she would sit before their fireplace with her feet on the bumper, drinking tea.

"You've no idea what a relief it is to come here, Arthur. You and Evelyn are not the burden that my family is."

Arthur sat in the chair opposite her, balancing a cookie on the edge of his saucer.

"I don't think my own children would agree with you. The other day the baby nearly decapitated herself with a tray of paint. Cried for over an hour," he said, whisking the crumbs from his lap into the fire. "I'm quite certain the whole thing has scarred her for life."

Albra smiled. "I shall be sure to tell them when they're older just how lucky they are to have you."

"Promise?"

"Certainly."

"Then you may have another cookie."

She laughed at this and took one anyway.

"How is your new studio?" she asked between bites.

Arthur frowned. "You're not trying to ruin my amusing mood are you?"

Albra turned back to her tea. "Just friendly inquiry."

"Have you thought about my offer?"

Evelyn was pregnant again and to cut back on their expenses, Arthur had given up his former studio. The switch from his loft to a small sitting room in his apartment had not been easy. The move forced Arthur to get rid of a number of his own paintings faster than he had intended, and he'd decided to place several pieces at an upcoming showing.

At Evelyn's prompting, he had asked Albra to join him.

"I told you, I don't paint for other people."

"Nonsense," he dismissed. "You don't mean it; I've seen the way you take criticism. Besides, that's a self-righteous and bourgeois attitude."

"Good," she said. "Those are two of my most appealing features."

After that they sat in silence, watching the fire. Albra found her gaze drawn to a small ember in the corner of the pit, and the orange glow inside its husk of carbon sputtered and began to fade. An instant later it was gone, lost among the larger blaze.

Soon, Evelyn came into the room and joined them. She was almost five month's pregnant and had begun feeling the awkwardness of her condition.

"Move over, you two," she muttered, abandoning herself into an adjacent chair. "It's taking longer and longer for that child to get to sleep . . ." her voice trailing off into a sigh.

"I was just asking Arthur here about his new studio," Albra commented.

"Oh yes," Evelyn rolled her eyes. "It was working out wonderfully until the baby nearly died under an avalanche of his things."

Arthur gave a mock frown. "This story becomes more dramatic each time you tell it."

Albra half-listened as the two talked together, their voices instinctively lowered for the sleeping child.

It would be nice, Albra thought, to have one's own home. Yet she knew even as she thought about it that it was impossible; this was not one of her choices. And her choices scared her terribly. The narrow world she had nurtured for so long was now crumbling perceptibly around her, and its eventual collapse was no longer something she could ignore. All around were signs of erosion and decay: the waves of something greater than herself, greater than all the assurances of the past, ate away at the fringe of her vision. Nothing lay untouched; no object, no relationship remained unmolested by the advance of that tide. Left in its wake was a world made cruel and barren, outside the comfortable agonies of her youth. She could almost convince herself that it was an illusion, a meaningless dream, like those she used to have. Sitting there before a winter fire with Arthur and Evelyn's voices hovering in its dim glow, she could almost believe the world was a fair place to live.

Evelyn glanced at Albra across the room. "I'm making more tea."

Albra lifted her feet from the bumper, blinking away her thoughts. "No, thank you," smiling faintly. "I should be going."

"Already?" Arthur seemed miffed.

"They'll need me before supper."

"How is everyone?" Arthur asked, handing her her coat.

"Not so well. Thank you both for the visit. I'm sorry to be such a bore . . ."

"Not at all," Evelyn put one hand on her stomach. "Come earlier if you can next time, and we can talk before the child's nap."

"Yes, of course."

"By the way," Arthur said. "I'm planning a little trip this summer with some of the others. Why don't you come along?"

Albra only nodded, though inside she was shocked by the sudden yearning she felt at the idea of getting away.

Half an hour later, she stepped off the trolley not far from her home. Around her the city was still and dark.

"Where has my strength gone?" She said this out loud, as though hoping a reply might be hiding somewhere.

Evelyn had taken her four or five times to the meetings down by City Hall. Albra had listened to the speeches and even handed out leaflets. Liberty was a popular word in 1920, and it had slipped eagerly from her tongue with the comfortable lubrication of innocence. Yet now that she was faced with something like it, Albra suddenly found herself aching inside for oppression. But why, she asked herself, why should I want misery?

Albra stirred from the silence of her melancholy. Here and there small fragments of snow began falling from the dark limbs of trees. Diving headlong into the night, they broke apart on bushes and roofs, careening into the unforgiving street.

∞

His appearance always shocked Mary, though by the second summer she knew what to expect. Standing at the window, she would watch him winding his way through the people in the street, and an almost-forgotten warmth would pass over her. It was only when he waved that she could be sure it was him, and all at once she would shudder with something close to fear. Then, with unseen restraint, she held out herself for this man at the door wanting to embrace her with what was a near-ly-expired claim to her body.

How she hated her son at that moment—hated the boy's self-conscious longing for something she could never again give him, hating herself for the denying of it, and hating all the more that shrouded voice inside that condemned her.

"It is good to see you," she would say. "Yes, it is good to have you home." And in the end she hated herself even more for meaning it.

Used to the open spaces of the vineyard, in the apartment Gabe now seemed like a bull in a china shop. For the first few days she would laugh at his awkwardness, but beneath her strained amusement lay a sense of panic and remorse. Gabe did not fit here, and it was never long before his confined energy ruptured the pattern of his mother's home.

One morning, shortly after dropping off the previous day's laundry, Gabe picked up soap from the grocer. It was not much out of his way, stopping to talk with one of the boys who worked behind the counter. When he arrived home, he was met by Mona who upbraided him for taking so long.

"Where did you get to? I've been waiting here all morning for you to bring that soap!"

He only looked at her, more startled than annoyed. "Here," he said handing it to her. "Next time get it yourself."

"That's a fine answer coming from you. I can't finish the day's scrubbing until you find time to get soap, and now I'm to do that, too?"

"Whose money do you think bought that soap? Did that come from the pittance you been earning all summer while I'm away? If it were up to you, we'd be eating cabbage morning and night."

Mary, who had kept quiet so far, looked up over the sheet she was wringing. "You're wrong, Gabe."

He paused, stunned by the sound of her voice. "What?"

"You're wrong about that. The girl mayn't earn as much as you, but between your train fare and tobacco and I don't know what else, there's more of her pay ending up on that dinner table than yours."

Gabe flinched noticeably. "How can you say that?"

Mary stopped what she was doing. "I'm not saying we don't appreciate what you bring in. But it isn't right for you to make out like it's more than it is."

Mona looked down at her feet with uncharacteristic modesty. "You just shouldn't keep us waiting," she said. "It's holding up our work. And work is money."

Gabe flushed mutely, turning back to a pile of ladies underwear on his ironing table.

That evening, when the laundry had been folded and wrapped with brown paper and twine, Gabe left the apartment to sulk in the chill October solitude. As he sat down on the curb, he found himself alone with the smell of leaves and late meals. To these he contributed the more amiable odour of his pipe, watching as the indeterminate trails of smoke faded into the shadows. His mother's apartment sat on a hill looking over the east half of the city and down to the bay. It was a clear night, and from where he sat Gabe could see the lights of Toronto flickering across the lake. Gabe often spent evenings in this way, braving the frost and drizzle to sit and look over the lake at the distant city. His brother lived there now, though Hal rarely came home more than politeness demanded.

Despite the relief he felt at being outside, Gabe's lips still worked nervously around the mouth of his pipe. Though he enjoyed the thing, it made him as self-conscious as a new hair-cut. His mother had been furious with it, and forbade him from smoking inside on account of the laundry.

"I'll not send back clean clothes smelling of the pool hall," she'd warned.

In the end, Gabe found he enjoyed the excuse to go out-side.

When the pipe had burned out, he emptied the black shards of tobacco into the gutter. He ran a hand through his hair with an agitated frown. His mother's criticism had left his stomach feeling hollow and dry. Never had she sided with Mona against him. The worst of it, though, was that he knew she was right. Yet the rush of guilt he felt was checked by sud-den indignation, a feeling of betrayal that hardened him like frost.

After coming home that autumn, Gabe had found working over the laundry almost unbearable. In hope of freeing himself from his mother's regime, he had turned to the congested string of steel mills about the harbour. But after the War, the few jobs that came up were taken by veterans. Those that did speak with him seemed indignant with his lack of experience.

"What do you know about working in a mill?"

Gabe had shrugged and tried to look confident. "My dad worked 'em."

"What's his name?"

"Thomas Oban."

The face blinked two or three times. "Never heard of him."

Gabe's heart sank. "He was at another mill," the boy explained.

An empathetic nod. "Lots of other mills . . . why not try your dad's?"

"Sure I will."

His father's mill? He had met his boss, even, and what good had it done? It seemed odd when he thought about it after, the mill owner wanting to meet him. But at the time he had been hopeful, taking it as a good sign.

"You say he worked here?"

"He ran one of the furnaces."

The gaze tightened, neck and shoulders pulled back in a coil. "Oban was it?"

"Yes."

"His name was Thomas?"

Gabe felt the despair at the top of his throat. "That's right."

A thin line melted its way up the man's jaw. "We haven't seen much of your father."

The boy gaped with hope. "You remember him, then?"

"Vaguely."

There was a strained moment as each waited for something more.

Gabe sighed unconsciously, and as he rose to leave his eye caught something embroidered on the man's cuff.

"Pryce? You're Mr. Pryce?"

The thin lips curled above his teeth. "Who'd you think I was?"

"It's not that," noting a crease in the man's shirt. "Only I never realized . . ." Gabe shrugged innocently and left, forgetting to close the door behind him.

Gabe knew the name already. It was marred by unfortunate odours, a name of yellowed undergarments, of wrested bits of hair, wrinkled collars, and the exhausted crust of semen.

It was bread crumbs and stale perfume. It was a gravy stain. The only face he had ever been able to put to the name was the extinguished complexion of a woman and the sound of three coins rubbing together in her outstretched hand. After the dirty water had been thrown out and the iron cooled, the name Pryce was as faceless as the starched collars that Gabe handed to Penny Pryce each Thursday before noon.

November has never been a generous month, marred by endless rain and naked trees, their black limbs stretching towards the grey horizon. When the showers cleared, Gabe took the opportunity to step out and stare at the stars as he had done as a boy. A handful of people made their way home, and he watched them now moving up the street. He was vaguely interested in the women ambling home, but his eye always seemed to latch onto a certain type. One could still tell who they were even without the armbands. For the most part, they worked somewhere in the city, either as shop girls, or secretaries, or teachers. But they had been marked out from the rest. It was something in the stare, he decided, something gone from the eyes. The War had taken something permanent from them: a child, a sweetheart.

And so when Ruby Parker walked up the hill toward him, Gabe already knew more than a little about her, even before recognizing her as the woman living next to his mother. As she approached him, Gabe stepped off the curb so as to put himself in her path.

Seeing an obstacle, the woman looked up defiantly as though ready to snap at him for blocking her way. Her stare stunned Gabe who gaped back, still unsure of what to say.

"Hello," was all he could muster.

The woman blinked. "What?"

Gabe cleared his throat and tried again.

She was not that old, he noticed. She had a compact face that had to be looked at for some time before it became pleasant. On her head she wore a green knitted cap that strained to contain the brown hair that peaked restlessly from beneath it. The rest of her was smothered in a coat of dull plaid. Despite this neglected appearance, something was unyielding, even strident, about the way she carried herself that left Gabe admiring her.

"Well, then," she said in her laconic way. "I'll be along."

Gabe watched as she slipped through the evening shadows and into the building.

From that day, Gabriel Oban and Ruby Parker met occasionally in the street or the dreary hallway that connected their lives. These were polite encounters during which neither person seemed to know what to do about the other's presence. But gradually these meetings became longer, until a friendship of sorts grew between the two.

She asked after his life, his work and family, but Gabe found his own existence a thing of discomfort. How could he speak to her of things he would not show himself? So instead he tried to deflect her interest in what already passed for a predictable and inbred existence.

Standing over his iron at the window, he might glance out at the winter sun slipping beneath the city, and recognize the solitary posture of Ruby passing beneath a lamp post. If he were nearly done starching the pile of other men's collars, Gabe would slip out into the cold to meet her.

"You're late today, Ruby."

"What are you doing out here without a proper hat?"

Gabe grinned at this, stuffing his hands in his coat pockets to preserve the warm feeling about his chest.

"Just come out for a smoke."

"Men have the stupidest ideas of entertainment."

"Well, it's just something small. Better than the bottle . . ." He broke off here, and the wind seemed all the colder.

"Why not smoke inside?"

Gabe looked at her through the chill gloom and shivered.

"Mother don't let me. Says it stinks up the laundry."

"Well you're welcome at my place. Frank used to; so did my dad. Mom was a real particular sort and only allowed him a pipe. So I guess I like the smell."

"Yes," he said. "A pipe's good."

"Your dad smoke?"

Gabe frowned. "Yes."

Ruby looked about her. "Well, you can come inside if you want."

Gabe looked down at the slush stuck to his feet. "Sure."

Ruby's apartment was smaller than the one his mother rented. There were two rooms, a kitchen and bedroom, joined by a small hallway. It was not particularly neat, the way Gabe had imagined it. The eye stuck on things: a stocking protruding from under a chair, half a cup of tea, the bits of meaningless clutter his mother had never allowed.

As they entered, she took off her coat and pointed to a chair.

"There," she said, still out of breath from the stairs. "You can smoke here if it suits you."

"Suits me fine," he said, trying to sound calm.

At that she went into the other room, only to return a moment later. "Have you eaten?"

"Yes," he lied. "But if you're going to eat I can leave."

"I don't mind."

"Okay, then."

Their conversation was stilted now in unfamiliar surroundings, and it took Gabe four attempts to light his pipe. But as the odour of food began to fill the tiny apartment they settled into an unruffled silence. It wasn't long before Gabe stood and said good bye, carrying her smile all the way down the hall.

Even though Gabe and Ruby were still uncertain of the emotional flavour of their friendship, it was clear Mary Oban found the match unpalatable. Though terrified by the upheaval he brought to her precarious world, Mary felt again the old determination to keep the boy from others. The presence of Ruby Parker now sent a fear into her that she did not understand, leaving her with only a ferocious desire to protect what was hers—just as she had that day so long ago in the garden.

More than once Mary watched the two from her kitchen window, sensing some new faculty in her son's body. It was like watching him grow a new limb. But Ruby exhibited no such clumsiness, did not stagger under the unwieldy burden of emotion. Nothing was contrived in the girl's appearance, nothing false. Only the weary amusement of someone who knows the path she is on, like a parent taking a child to his first summer fair.

When Gabe entered the apartment he found his mother sitting beside a stack of finished laundry. She was almost smiling.

"I was just wondering where you'd got to."

"Out for some air."

"Mona's already eaten, but I decided to hold off till you came home."

Gabe nodded hesitantly. "Want me to heat it up?"

"It's alright. I'll get to that in a minute."

"I'm famished."

"I should say so. All that fresh air after a day of working."

"I'm hungry," he repeated.

Mary stood and went into the kitchen, talking to him over her shoulder. "Still snowing out there?"

Gabe looked out the window. "Yup."

"I thought maybe it had stopped."

"It's been coming down all evening."

"You look a little dry for being outside in this weather."

Gabe was quiet for a moment. "Met Mrs. Parker on the stoop coming in."

"Mrs. Parker?"

"Yeah, Ruby."

"Ruby is it?"

"You know her name, Mother."

"I suppose I did."

Mona coughed somewhere in the apartment.

Gabe began flipping through a newspaper.

"You spent all that time talking on the stoop, did you?"

"She invited me inside to smoke."

"That's nice for you, isn't it? Better than a saloon I should think, and legal too. I'm sure it's a real inconvenience for her, with the smell. You know how I feel about it."

"Actually she doesn't mind."

Mary was quiet for a long time in the kitchen, and when she called him for dinner Gabe's fingers were dark with ink from reading the paper.

"Do you ever wish you'd gone to school?" Mary asked suddenly.

"No." Gabe looked at her over his meal.

"I just thought you might have felt lonely sometimes. Not being around anyone your age."

"There was Hal and Mona."

"Yes, that's true." She poured them both mugs of tea. "I was just afraid I'd done wrong keeping you at home." Mary smiled absently. "Your father wasn't for it, you know? No, he wanted you to go to school with the other boys."

Gabe listened as he ate.

"I wasn't prepared to let you die, you know. A mother doesn't give up her children that easily," she said, fiercely sipping her tea. "Almost killed me when Hal enlisted. But your father wouldn't hear of him staying. I was so sure he wouldn't go, you see. I thought nothing was stronger than a mother's will. But the War was stronger. As though being a boy meant he had to go get killed."

The whole time Gabe sat gazing at his mother's hand. He reached forward and touched her softly.

"Thank God," she whispered. "I know it's silly, but I used to lie awake thinking that God would take him. He'd saved one of my children already, and I thought I'd no right asking Him to save another." Mary smiled at Gabe. "It doesn't matter that Hal won't come home anymore. He's alive. Still, sometimes it's like he never returned from the War. He was in such a hurry to leave as soon as he returned."

"Yeah, but you know why," he asked, his eyes confiding in her. "You can't blame him after what happened."

The muscles in Mary's arm tightened. "Why can't I? Don't I have the right to expect more from my son than I do from his father?"

Gabe withdrew his hand.

"Should I expect him to repeat his father's sins? Is that why I gave him life? To be no better than the last one? Every mother wants her sons to be better than her husband. So don't go expecting me to think different because your father was so particularly weak!" With that Mary pushed by her son and slammed the door to her bedroom.

The next day was a Friday and Ruby Parker was late coming home from work. Reaching the top of the stairs she was surprised to meet Mary Oban on the landing.

"Is that you, Mrs. Oban? What're you doing out here in the hallway?"

"I came to have a word, Mrs. Parker."

"Oh." Ruby faltered with her key. "Will you come in?"

"It won't take but a minute."

Ruby licked her lips. "What can I do for you?"

Mary went right to the point. "Leave him be."

"I'm sorry?"

"You know what I mean."

"You're referring to Gabe?"

"My son."

"I don't understand."

"I think you do."

Ruby shook her head, blushing in the half-light of the hallway.

"He's not for you."

"And who are you to make such a decision?"

"I'll not have it."

"I beg your pardon!" The end of the key bit angrily into her palm. "I'm insulted."

"I don't care for your feelings one bit," Mary spat at her feet. "What happens to you means nothing compared to that boy."

Ruby groped for the composure to sneer. "Boy?"

Mary lifted her chin slightly and brought her hand hard across the woman's face.

"You've no right . . ."

Ruby choked on her shock, staggering. Though shorter than Ruby, Mary stood completely aware of her own capacities.

It was a moment before Ruby could speak.

"I'm going, I'm going to, to . . ."

Mary narrowed her gaze. "You'll what?"

"I'm going to tell him."

But in that moment a muffled sound came from behind Mary's door, and a dark smile passed over her face.

"He's not for you!" she hissed again.

In the spring of 1921, the slow, leaking away of Calvin's life quite suddenly became a flood that swept up the lives of his wife and daughter.

Hannah caught a cold that winter that wouldn't seem to leave her, and Elizabeth took her into her own home to let her recuperate. Though Julius looked in every day, Albra was left alone now in the great house to care for her father. Death was close, and Albra often shuddered at its proximity.

At first she had resisted his pleas, but then a truck had appeared and a man approached the back door with a crate under one arm. In the end, he only shook his head and left the bottles there on the stoop.

"He's paid for 'em in advance," the man said over his shoulder.

After he had gone, Albra stood looking at the bottles. The neighbours might see, she thought, trying to halt her fleeing strength. And so she had brought them into the house, shaking with remorse.

Pouring out the liquor for her father, Albra became panicked.

"What are you doing?" she asked herself, even as her fingers put the cork back in the bottle. "You can't do this; not the way he his now," and she watched as her legs carried her up the stairs to his study. "You're going to kill him," she hissed desperately, just as her hand reached for the door knob. Then, stepping into the room she heard him stir in his bed next to her.

Those eyes. Albra loathed them. The way they captured her, gutting her like some fish. Leaving only the meat. Standing just outside of their circumference, she watched them search the ceiling's emptiness. Looking for her.

"Here," she said, finally. "Drink this."

To distract herself, Albra set up an easel in her father's room, working in the afternoons when he slept. Though exhausted, Albra found a curious energy here as the odour of paint mingled with those of unguents and bedpans. As evening descended, she would set out candles, filling the room with their shivering glow, giving her painting an atmosphere of memory, of excavation.

When her father woke, they would talk together through the encroaching shadows.

"I am lost," he told her, and her brush shook a little as he spoke.

"You should rest," she said.

"No one will remember me. I'll be forgotten."

"That's not true; now try to sleep and maybe you'll feel better."

But he persisted, his head rocking back and forth on the pillow as he spoke. "Who will know that I lived? I have left nothing. Soon there will be no trace of me. I will be reduced to a piece of stone with a few scratches on it."

"That's right," she replied abruptly, putting down her brush. "You will have no more than the rest of us."

The man closed his eyes for a moment while his tongue worked mutely behind his lips. Albra blushed with a sudden rush of anger, and it suddenly occurred to her that she might just let him die. Let him die without ever lifting another finger in his direction. But when he looked at her again it was with the pleading gaze of a child. Despite the disfigurement of terror and illness, in the old man's gaze was the shadow of a younger face. She longed to hold his sagging head at her breast, to save him as he had her. But of course she was no mother; Death bowed not to her.

"It has all been so, so little. So much compromise; so much wasted and taken away out of avarice and weakness. Beware of weakness. Watch or it will latch upon you like some pleasant vampire and consume your dreams."

Albra bristled suddenly, remembering that face beneath the train with its cry, reaching out like Paul had done across the chasm that separates the living and the dead. Then, looking down at him, she grew cold and her voice became venomous. "You're not talking again of that ridiculous time with mother in Greece are you?"

He turned his head at this to look at her.

"How dare you!" he hissed.

She turned back to her work in a rough jerking manner as though part of her resisted the motion.

"You did as you pleased," she said finally. "We all do exactly as we please."

He picked up a glass beside his bed and hurtled it at her. "What kind of child are you? Bring me something! I'm a sick man, for God's sake!"

Calvin's hands shook on top of the sheets, and his scabbed flesh seemed to glow slightly with his rage.

"I'm not going anywhere while you talk to me in that manner," she snapped. But after a moment she went anyway and brought him back a glass filled almost to the brim.

In this way, Albra spent the last of his days, torn by altering impulses to either nurse and comfort the man, or to cast him off. The violence of these emotions shook her, and as she had in the years that followed Paul's death, Albra lived in awe of the terrible assurances that came with each.

One day she set aside her brush and slipped out to make herself something warm to drink. She was gone only twenty minutes or so, scrubbing the paint from her fingers while she waited for the water to boil. But when Albra came back into the room, the sight of her father made her drop the cup she was holding.

Calvin lay with his head to one side.

For Albra, what came next would always remain confused and terrible, with faces and events all pushed together like a broken jigsaw. Julius arrived. There were loud noises: the rapid tread of feet along the halls, the shutting of doors.

Sorting the pieces of this time in her head, it seemed to Albra that the one constant through it all—the thread—was the man's death wail. For hours, he seemed to scream out with all his might, oblivious to the sedative Julius gave him. It was a piercing, savage sound. A testament to Life's infinite indifference.

Among those who came to comfort the dying man, only his youngest daughter remembered that cry and where she had first heard it. It touched something hidden inside Albra, the echo of a voice beyond the edge of her memory. The sound of her father's cry came as a final blow to some enclave, some rampart of secreted credulity that she had stored away through all that had happened. Inside her, his voice formed a small hole that went right through her and began to grow, sucking her into herself.

For two full days, they laboured over the dying man, pausing now and then when the morphine took effect to gather themselves. But when he woke again, it was always with a sudden shriek, jarring them.

Toward the end of the second day, Calvin Creighton grew silent. His breathing became difficult and irregular, and his eyes glazed with immeasurable distance. Julius saw each of these things in their turn with calm certainty. When it was time, he touched his wife gently on the palm to let her know.

"You should wake your sister," he said.

When Albra came into the study, she saw how still Julius stood, and something inside her gripped itself into a fist.

"Your father has died," he said. "You should be proud of him. His spirit was willing, but his body was too weak."

"You are wrong," she replied. "The flesh isn't ever weak."

With that she collapsed on the floor at their feet.

Gabe sat with the others by their bunkie, listening as they talked of their work and the wine it would bring. Only a handful had been asked to stay on through the winter and there was now a restlessness about the circle of tired limbs which flexed with anticipation. They shared an exaggerated closeness at these times. An arm was thrown with significant carelessness across one's shoulders, and each breeze seemed to carry up a whisper of voices from the orchard.

Gabe, however, felt apart from those around him. Wresting himself from the tangle of people, he stepped out past the haze of grey pipe smoke that glided up from their gathered voices. It was near dark by then, and as he walked down into the vineyard the whole valley seemed to stretch beyond his vision into the fading orange light. Ahead of him, a woman's figure stepped lightly up the path, her hair damp and long from washing. Gabe smiled at her with difficulty. He had noticed this woman before, but inside him something shrank at the thought of speaking to her so he kept his eyes on the path.

At the bottom of the hill he stopped by the stream. Kneeling, he scooped up a handful of water and let it run between his fingers and over his head. Against his leg Gabe felt an awkward jab, and reaching into his pocket he pulled out a carefully folded envelope.

Two days ago he had written to tell his mother he would be staying on with the vintner. He would be home, he had written, but only for Christmas this year. Between the single sheet of paper he had left nearly all his wages from that summer. It would be enough, he knew. Still, he hesitated with the thought that something obscure and irreversible hid between those folds of paper.

He sighed and turned back to the stream. As he sat washing himself, the night grew noticeably still. From the hills, gaunt patches of mist began rising above the vines.

The next night, Gabe sat in the shade of a lopsided apple

tree, the tail of a cat passing against his leg. Men brought beer in large open boxes heavy with ice. People hot from dancing passed around him, their skin damp and trembling from the touch of bodies. Drinking from a clay bowl, Gabe smiled unconsciously at the music and voices that enclosed him, his head nodding gently with alcohol and the sway of the dancers. A gleeful numbness swept over him like wood smoke, and soon he no longer felt the heavy sag of the envelope in his pocket. About him the world lay gilt in an amber glow of fire.

Contemplating the wine in his dish, Gabe was struck by his own face looking back at him. "Look at me," he said to his reflection.

A lamb was killed somewhere behind the trees, and three men set to work putting it on a spit and roasting it. Someone passed Gabe a piece of meat hanging from one of the ribs. Squatting among the crowd, he gorged himself with a sudden and violent hunger, watching as avenues of grease seeped between his fingers.

Later, when the sun had gone, he danced with the others around an immense fire of dead vines. The music came instinctively to him, each pulse as familiar and expected as his own heartbeat. Now an appendage of the drums, his feet and shoulders responded to each beat with primitive thrusts. Against him brushed the hands and hips of other workers. With each new contact, his skin bristled at the thrill, the sensuality of tribal communion. More wine appeared and soon he found the woman from the stream, and they danced together in the cascading shadows of fire.

Caught by the music, the coals seemed to vomit forth sparks to the drum's pulse. Sitting precariously on a donkey, Lambro leaned forward to grab lecherously at the dancers. Singing as he moved, Gabe drew instinctively closer to the girl's body. Her arms were hot and strong across his neck, and in her eyes he found the reflection of himself. Beside them leapt a woman with broad naked buttocks carrying a child above her head. At her side thrust the limbs of her husband, also naked, his back streaked with muscle and fire.

About midnight, as the flames consumed the last vine, the large boxes were brought into the light by four men wearing only their shirts wrapped about them as loin cloths. From beyond the circle of fire the drums stopped. The dancers, as though recognizing some signal, abruptly calmed and stood about the fierce glow of coals. Against his arm Gabe felt the girl's waist loosen and still. Then all at once, lifting the boxes nearly over their heads, the men emptied the melted ice onto the fire, sending forth a hiss that blew ash and steam into the sudden darkness. Instantly, cheering rose above the vineyard. For the first time Gabe noticed the stillness about him, and as the sweat cooled against his skin he became conscious of the darkness, the echo of voices, and the slowing cadence of his own breathing.

Gabe felt the girl drawing him into the fields of newly planted vines which stretched out indefinitely beneath the balm of moonlit clay. The leaves brushed against his arms as he passed, wetting him with the chill dew until his shirt was soaked through. Soon he became aware of insects calling to one another in the stillness, and beyond the pale silhouette of the pressing barns came the lazy clap of a door shutting. Gabe paused, squeezing the warm knot where their hands met.

"Here?" he whispered, grasping in the night for her other hand.

Somewhere among the rows they lay together on the cooling soil, each reaching out into darkness.

The next morning Gabe woke before the others. Stretching luxuriously under his sheets, he paused a moment to watch as the dawn crept across the floor. Rising, he dressed and stepped out into the pale blue light, which cut across the tops of the apple trees where dew still hung like pregnant bees from each leaf. Passing quickly through the valley, he turned onto the gravel road, a small tail of dust following him all three miles to the post office in town.

ॐ

Little more than the foundation endured. Over the years, the remaining timber and stone had been pilfered or burned. Soon, weeds reclaimed all but the cellar floor, which lay gutted and opened to the sky like a tongueless mouth. The site had become known among the men travelling the rail lines in search of work. At night, their cooking fires shone an eerie glow up the bare limestone of the chimney, which pointed like an accusing finger at the stars.

Had Earl Pryce known his farm was being used by tramps, he would probably not have put a stop to it. After the night of his party, Earl never set foot again on the land, but instead had his secretary draft a letter giving Jarvis Mekes free rein upon it.

Despite the farmer's honest efforts, the farm remained the only unprofitable investment Pryce had ever made, sucking money each season into the unyielding soil. Yet the steady drain of capital went, like a leech's appetite, almost unnoticed among the colossal limbs of Leda Steel.

There was a lag in business after the War ended, but within a year of the armistice his mill had been re-equipped to accommodate domestic markets. For that small period, hesitancy spread within the great plants stretching out along the harbour, an anxiety and vacillation they had never known before.

For a brief instant, the world seemed unclear. But before long the great engines of steel gave a sigh of relief, and in a wink sanity descended with treacherous significance upon the city. Once again, the earnest sense of purpose carried men to work. Each hour seeped guilelessly back into their lives, supporting the motions of existence. It became the currency of time, and thus thought itself eternal.

The gulls that populated the waterfront looked on each day at the busy scurry about the yards and inside the furnace rooms. Soaring high overhead, the birds warily avoided the stacks of fire and smoke, though impatience occasionally provided an unwary Icharus.

From his own perch, Earl Pryce watched the labour of Leda Steel. Below him, the beady figures of men weaved across the loading docks. Pursing his lips thoughtfully, he gazed upon their backs striped with coal dust and sweat, noting the careful strain with which they loaded each ingot. He saw with perfect clarity how it was, how much of himself had gone into filling each mould. Yet, for all that, he could not touch the thing itself. Earl's gaze narrowed upon a man standing by the furnace door, his face swollen and red from the heat.

They would never own anything, Earl thought, but still they could castrate me.

They were bound to each other in hopeless dependence, like soil and seed. And the bond tormented them all.

six

Following her father's death, Albra thought she would never paint again, but with spring the dark orchid of grief beneath her chest had begun to wilt. After the funeral, Elizabeth and Julius moved into the family home on Stibbard Avenue. Hannah had invited the move, as if anxious to fill the house again with people and life, but for Albra it came too soon. One afternoon she came home to find Julius had taken over her father's study, and that her own room was being refurbished as the nursery.

"I hope you don't mind," Elizabeth had said. "It's the farthest from mother's room and we don't want her woken up by the baby."

"Why should that matter?" Albra snapped. "Crying never bothered her when we were children."

Elizabeth set her smile firmly, ignoring the comment. "Julius and I are so looking forward to having you with us. You'll be such a help raising the children."

"What do you mean?"

Elizabeth's back straightened, and a cool enamel passed

over her eyes. "I just assumed. What else have you to do now that father's gone?"

"No," she said, hardening. "I shall be busy with my own affairs," and at that moment her painting seemed the most important thing in the world.

Ironically, all this was thrust from Albra's mind a few days later when Arthur's wife went into labour. A friend of Evelyn's named Sophia arrived to assist with the birth. Arthur sat with his wife until her suffering became too much, and Sophia sent him out.

"Why did you do that?" Albra gasped.

"He was only getting in our way. Now," she said, turning to Evelyn, "let's finish this and get that child out of there."

The next two hours seemed to Albra a kind of dream—part nightmare, part miracle. Between spasms, Evelyn's gaze sometimes fell on her, and each time Albra was appalled at the naked sincerity that pain can bring between two people. Swathed in this woman's agony, Albra felt herself included in some marvel, some horrible ritual of which she had never been aware. It was the first time since her brother's death that she had felt with someone else's body rather than her own.

Albra stayed on with Evelyn and Arthur for another two months, lending a hand with the baby and sacrificing none of the dignity that doing it for Elizabeth would have. At the end of two months, however, Albra returned to her mother's house, uncertain of the life which awaited her.

Resisting the servitude that Albra had seen in her sister's plans was not easy. It began with unannounced favours. At first Albra tried convincing herself that the growing requests were insignificant, but one morning, when she found a list of errands sitting on her breakfast plate, she knew it had gone too far. When Elizabeth came home that afternoon, she was annoyed to find her sister painting on the verandah.

"I haven't had a free minute all day."

"But you're painting?"

"Precisely."

"Surely you could make time for a few . . ."

"Not today."

"What? You have no responsibilities, no family or house to care for, you have no friends beside those gypsies you're always on about! Am I to presume that amid this hectic schedule of yours there is no time to help your sister with her child?"

Albra set down her brush. "You didn't even ask me!"

"Well, if you would get up earlier, perhaps you'd be able to discuss the day over breakfast like the rest of us."

"When I get up is my concern; changing diapers is yours!"

Elizabeth flinched at the retort. "Don't think you can act the way you did when Father was alive. If you were my daughter, I would have spanked that spark right out of you. It may be precocious and endearing at twelve, my dear; but at your age it's a poor picture indeed. Everyone sees through your artistic posturing. Look about you. You're an unconnected, plain, presumptuous woman who dabbles in painting."

"That's right," Albra hissed, tears streaking her face. "But you can't figure out why you're jealous!"

And so when Arthur offered her the chance to join a group of his friends in the country, Albra jumped at the opportunity to escape.

"You don't mind going?" he asked.

"I'm like a bruise there," she said. "I remind them of all we've been through."

From the start, it was everything Albra had hoped for. They drove along the lake to get there, through farms and villages that were little more than a few houses gathered at a crossroad. They stayed on a farm belonging to a brother of one of the artists and within a day or two each person had settled into a private routine. But at night everyone came together again, the men smoking and playing cards in loud voices while the women sat on the porch. Albra floated between each group, comfortable with them both.

Despite the holiday atmosphere of the place, there was a quiet focus among the painters that bordered on anxiety.

"We are here to work," Arthur assured her.

And so, following their lead, Albra left each morning lugging her things along dirt roads and fence lines until she came upon something that interested her. To start, she sketched or painted the natural things around her: fields of hay, a calf searching for its mother, a bumblebee atop a daisy. But these scenes soon became unpleasant.

In despair she showed what she had done to Evelyn.

"You didn't do badly with the calf," she said. "Why don't you try something more animate? You've always done better with portraits."

Albra took her advice. One night she woke to find Evelyn feeding her child, and the image impressed itself upon Albra's gaze. Snatching up her pencil, she quickly sketched the two by candlelight, ignoring Evelyn's protests.

"It was your idea," Albra countered. "The least you can do is support it."

The next day, Albra found a shaded spot beneath some trees, and began painting from the sketch she had done. Arthur soon came over to see her progress.

"Moving a little slow, aren't you?"

"I'm having trouble starting," she said.

She remembered all the paintings of nursing mothers—those pie-faced innocents of mail-order porcelain—all seeming so virginal. Studying her sketch again, Albra remembered back to the night the child was born: the screams splintering with exhaustion, begging for the end, for birth.

Albra decided she could not paint what she saw, but rather what she remembered. The two images—the one on the page and the one in her memory—merged together in a kind of reckoning between the heaven and hell of the thing. About Evelyn's mouth she now drew in the lines of agony, and from her breast a dribble of blood. The child, too, was amended. His mouth wrenched open with two fangs protruding like a vampire's.

When it was done Albra hesitated to show Evelyn.

"No," she said. "You were right to show me. That is how it is."

Arthur, however, had taken it quite differently. "That's offensive!" was his first response. "What are you trying to do here? Is this some new form of birth control?"

Albra shrugged. "It's what I see."

The others disapproved too, and over the next week Albra felt them tacitly change their attitude toward her. Where once they listened to her with a vague sort of politeness, she now caught some of the other artists staring at her when she spoke—listening and challenging what she said.

She mentioned this new distance to Evelyn, who smiled in an irritated and sympathetic way. "It's unfortunate that it has to be this way, but it's a good thing in the end. A man never really sees you until you tell him to go to hell."

☙

Late in the morning, a group of four or five people came along the road where Gabe and the others worked. Seeing them, the group skirted around the workers at a polite distance.

As they passed, Gabe noticed two of them break off from the group and sit in the shade of an immense elm. It seemed forward of them to sit there watching, but in a little while the work drew his attention away and he forgot about them. Gabe and the others were busy working a stretch of land by the road, clearing it for new vines. They were cutting and stacking brush in piles for burning.

When they stopped for lunch, there was a ripple of anxiety in the other men.

"Our food is under the tree there," one of them said.

"Well, go bring it here," another returned.

"I don't know about you," said Gabe, "but I intend to eat in the shade, guests or no guests."

That seemed to decide it for the rest, and they followed him over to the tree.

As he approached, Gabe saw that one of the figures was a woman, and he became suddenly indignant with her presence. The food was sitting in a canvas sack at the foot of the tree, and as he gathered it up the women addressed him.

"We're not going to disturb your lunch, I hope?"

Gabe could see she was young, about his age. Brown hair curling about her neck.

"Won't bother us," he said before turning to join the others.

After they ate, the men went back to work. Gabe set about burning the piles of brush they had collected, using the last of the kerosene from their lamps to start the fires. From the corner of his eye he watched the woman beneath the elm.

That night during dinner, Evelyn pointed out the flakes of ash clinging to Albra's hair.

"It must have been this afternoon," she explained. "We saw some men burning brush by the road."

"What were you doing there?"

"Working."

At Evelyn's request, Albra retrieved the large pad she used for drawing and showed her what she had been doing. The first sketches were of individual limbs and backs. Then, whole bodies began to appear in postures of unconscious intimacy: a man sharpening an axe, someone scratching the hair about his belly.

Albra blushed suddenly. "That one there," she whispered, "had hair everywhere!"

Evelyn paused as she turned to the last sketch. "What were you trying to do here?"

"Something experimental," she said. "Obviously it didn't work, but it was worth a try."

It was a sketch of the men eating, faces bleached and stoic in the sun. At the edge of the group one of the men sat half in darkness, shadow cutting a swath across his body.

"I botched this fellow," she explained. "I was trying to show his incompleteness. He seemed so different from the others."

The others. Albra had felt their eyes pushing her to the margin of their vision. But the small one, with the narrow chest, he did no such thing; his eyes hung back from her, traced the edge of her skirt but no farther. His gaze tentative but defiant. He had not liked her there any more than the others, she knew. But he had not tried to remove her with his eyes. He left her where she was.

That afternoon the men had followed a path along the river back to the vineyard, saws and axes thrown across their drooping shoulders. The face and chest of each man was black and creased with dirt and soot, and on the way they stopped to wash in the river. Despite the day's heat, the water was so cold it made the top of Gabe's head ache. But it was clean too, and they splashed about in it like boys, the scabs of sweat and filth peeling from their flesh.

They wrung the dirt from their clothes and hung them to dry.

That night Albra lay awake, watching clouds roll across the fields, lightning shuddering in the distance. Through the window she could see the fields suddenly illuminated before her. She stared until the storm had disappeared, leaving the sky clean and black.

The next afternoon, she returned to the elm tree only to find that the men had moved farther on, so she followed the sound of their voices until she found them. They were working along the edge of a hill clouded by smoke from their fires.

Albra sat at the crest of the slope for almost an hour, listening to the sound of the saws and the men singing. Not long after, a head emerged, rising up through the smoke. As he reached the top of the hill, he stopped to catch his breath, unaware that she was watching him. Concealed in the tall grass, Albra remained unnoticed as he strode past. She felt a sudden surge of power, like a lion observing its prey.

Up close there was more to him, Albra saw, than she had first thought. Standing there with his hands resting on his hips, chest streaked with grime and soot, he seemed more substantial. Behind the stubble and dirt was a kind of patient sadness, a resigned and enduring quality as if he were looking for something lost, something he was unlikely to find. She had seen this look in the men who came back from the War, staring this way at children or a pretty girl.

Stopping a little ways from where she sat, Gabe began dragging the larger branches back down the hill. As he turned to go, his eye snagged on her face peering out from the grass, and he stopped dead.

For a moment, the two stared at each other in silence.

"Are you alright?" he said, feeling annoyed.

"I was just sitting."

Gabe pointed to the large pad she held on her knees. "What's that?"

"Oh," she said, colouring. "I sometimes sketch things."

"Is that what you're doing?"

"I came to watch," she replied.

Gabe frowned. "Not much to see here," nodding at the

blue haze covering the slope below them. Then, as if to prove his point, he turned and disappeared into the smoke.

Gabe passed the other men who walked like phantoms among the orange glow of the fires. Heaving the branches he carried onto the nearest of these, Gabe stood back as the flames gorged on the dead bark and leaves, spitting out a canopy of ash that settled about him.

After that Albra came around often, sometimes bringing others who sat and painted with her. To the men clearing ground she became something they accepted almost without noticing, like a hawk watching from its perch. Finding Albra sitting on a rock or beneath a tree, they merely walked around her without looking up.

Gabe, however, could feel no such indifference around her. He did not know how to take her, recognizing her clothes and the cadence of her voice as marks of suspicion. Everything about her signalled to him the alien reality of the rich. He tried to imagine this woman meeting his mother, but each time the two images were incompatible.

What drew him to this woman through his own hostility, finally, was her obsession with the pictures she made. It was like coming upon someone staring into the sky. He looked and looked to see what captivated her. When the day's work was done, he would stop and speak with her, commenting at times on the sketch or painting she was working on. Once, she invited him to look through her sketching pad.

"Most of these are a little old," she said, as if by apology. "I didn't do anything for almost six months or so, and I didn't start working again until recently."

Gabe continued to examine the book as if he had not heard her. "It's strange," he said finally. "Most of these people are cripples . . ." and he showed her some of the sketches she had done: limbless veterans; old women with no teeth; children ruined from polio; tubercular beggars.

Albra took back her drawings. "I don't see your point."

Gabe looked at her hands, the long uncalloused fingers.

"I hope they don't make you work on Sundays," she said, her face almost hopeful.

"Only during the harvest."

"Do you ever go to the beach?"

"Yes, if it's hot."

"I'm going tomorrow with some friends."

Gabe looked down at his feet. They were quiet for a moment. Then Albra stood up to leave, brushing the grass from her skirt.

"Would you mind if I came with you?" he asked suddenly, his voice hoarse.

She stopped and looked him over, as if for the first time.

"That would be fine," she said finally. "We'll pack something to eat."

The next morning Gabe was waiting for her under the elm where they had first met.

"You bringing your things?" he said, pointing to the case of paints she carried. "Even to the beach?"

"One never knows when one will be inspired," she said, making an effort to sound convincing.

Albra was accompanied by Evelyn, Arthur, and their youngest child. Though it was early, the day was already hot, and the men opened their shirts to cool off. As they walked, Gabe stayed just ahead of them until Evelyn invited him to hold the baby.

"So Mr. Oban," Evelyn said beneath her wide-brimmed hat. "Can you suggest a good place for our picnic?"

"There's a place down the road that overlooks the beach. Good shade and a nice view."

"Sounds perfect," she answered. "Lead on!"

Albra smiled at Gabe, suddenly shy. She knew from the exuberant tone in Evelyn's voice that her friend approved of him.

Arthur, too, seemed comfortable around him, and offered Gabe a cigar by way of starting a conversation. Soon the two men were walking ahead, smoking and talking. Albra and Evelyn fell behind, immersed in their own conversation.

"So this is where you've been going for the last week," the older woman prodded.

Albra frowned. "No. At least not at first. It was all of them that interested me, the men that is. Well, you've seen the sketches yourself."

"I must admit," Evelyn smiled. "I wondered at this turn in your subject matter."

"But you," and Albra's voice became suddenly awkward, "you approve of this—I mean you don't think I'm out of my head do you?"

Evelyn smiled again, though more quietly this time, drawing her fingers through Albra's.

"There is nothing to worry about. You haven't done anything at all."

At this she turned and strode ahead, taking her husband's arm.

Reaching the top of a hill, they were met with a breeze coming off the lake. To the north, a dark line of cloud was advancing.

"Might rain," Gabe observed.

Arthur opened another button on his shirt, letting the breeze pass across his chest. "We could use the cooling off."

From here, Gabe led them off the road and down a lane overhung with red sumacs. Following a turn in the lane, they came to a derelict-looking farmhouse squatting in the shadow of a large barn.

Arthur stopped and looked at their guide.

"What's this?" he asked.

"No one lives here," Gabe explained. "It's all right."

"Where's the owner?" Albra asked.

Gabe turned and looked at her. "The War."

The others stared in silence at the old farmstead.

"It's okay," Gabe said again. "We can use the barn if you'd like. It looks right over the lake."

Arthur wiped the sweat from his face decisively. "Sounds good to me."

The barn stood open and as they approached a pair of swallows swept past them into the sun. They followed Gabe up a ladder to the loft where a loading door swung open onto the lake. The breeze hummed quietly through the plank walls of the barn, sending straw dancing about their feet. Below them, the barnyard stretched for almost a hundred yards before slipping down into dunes of sand that slid into the lake.

"What did I tell you?" Gabe said, obviously pleased.

"This is perfect!" Evelyn admitted.

"You sound surprised," he said.

"It is splendid," Albra interjected, laughing. "Besides, I trusted you all along."

"Well, it's almost noon," Arthur said. "Shall we eat first or swim?"

Albra took the baby who had been sleeping on Gabe's shoulder and laid him in the cool straw. "If it's all right with you I'd like to sit for a moment. We'll watch the baby and get lunch ready," she said. "You two go swim, and we'll go after."

When they had gone, Gabe stood in the doorway with his arms out, letting the breeze cool him. He waved to Evelyn and Arthur as they made their way across the sand.

Sitting beside the child, Albra stared shyly at Gabriel's back. Turning around, he stood in front of her, his face lost in shadow.

"I hope you drink wine," he said.

Albra blinked. "What?"

"I wanted to bring something to eat," he explained, reaching into a canvas bag he had been carrying over his shoulder. "But I've never been a cook."

He placed two bottles on the wooden floor.

"It's good wine," he assured her. "I helped make it," and Albra thought she saw his chest rise when he said this. "But if you're against that sort of thing. I mean, if you're not—"

Albra smiled kindly into the shadow of his face. "That was a lovely thing to bring," she said.

The intimacy in her voice left him feeling awkward again, and to shake the feeling he began to look about the loft. Along one wall hung a collection of implements, each scabbed with rust and neglect. Among these was a plough propped in the corner on its nose, and as he was about to move on, his eye caught something embossed on the metal: LS. Reaching out, he let his fingers trace each letter. Beneath his skin, the iron felt cold and still.

"Is there anything wrong?" Albra asked.

He paused for a moment, letting the distance between him and these letters settle back into place.

"No," he replied, shaking his head. "I know the men who made this. But that seems a long time ago."

At that moment, Albra stepped past him into the doorway, watching the horizon fill with cloud.

"Look," she said. "It's coming." And as she said this, the wind picked up, carrying the cool gusts of an approaching storm.

Gabe leaned against the door frame. Just then his eyes widened and he choked back a sudden laugh as he pointed toward the beach. Albra's reaction was one of speechless shock. Half-hidden in the long grass that grew up about the dunes, Arthur and Evelyn could be seen lying together in the sand.

At this moment, the storm seemed to descend upon them, and in an instant the sky let loose an applause of thunder and rain. From where they stood, Albra and Gabe looked on as husband and wife started to dress themselves. Having covered everything demanded by modesty, the two ran for proper shelter.

Albra turned and punched Gabe who had begun to laugh. "Stop that!" she insisted. "Those are my friends."

"Yes," he laughed. "Charming ones!"

Then, just as Albra was preparing a volley of invectives, she was distracted by the sound of laughter rising up through the floor. Looking down between the boards, Gabe and Albra watched as Arthur kissed his wife. Then, giggling to themselves, the couple finished dressing. When they climbed into the loft, Arthur and Evelyn found the two setting out lunch.

Surprised to find themselves so hungry, the four ate in silence, communicating only with grins and nods. Passing around a loaf of black bread, each person tore a crust from it, folding it around pieces of cheese and meat. Gabe managed to uncork the wine he brought and they took turns drinking from the bottles. Evelyn produced a half-crushed pie that they dove into, laughing at the blueberries that ran like syrup over their lips. Afterwards, they lay back in the hay watching Evelyn feed the baby and listening to the rain against the barn.

When the rain passed, Albra and Gabe walked down to the lake to swim. Using a dune well beyond the vantage of the barn, Gabe changed into the cut-down pants that served as his bathing trunks. He paused to look at himself before putting them on, his body bleached by the afternoon sun. And in that moment he tried—as he had so often as a boy—to see himself as others did; for the first time since he could remember, the thought brought no pain.

Tucking his shirt into his trunks, Gabe ran out onto the beach. Albra was already in the water, having stopped shoulder-deep in the lake, hesitating. Her back was to him as he ran along the shore to a gnarled willow that leaned over the water. Reaching it, he climbed onto one of its branches before leaping into the lake.

Albra heard a shriek, suddenly silenced as his body was swallowed by the waves. As the moment passed she was thrown head-long into some distant place, her body plunging beneath the surface, fingers reaching out into the darkness to touch him. When she reached the bottom, she looked up to see his body rising alone to the surface waiting for her to appear. And for a moment, Albra hovered in the water's embrace. Looking up, it occurred to her that she knew what Paul had seen at that moment of separation, and, more importantly, that this was as close as she would come to touching him.

Later, as they were gathering their things, it began to rain again. They chose to wait out the storm in the barn. Sitting together, they traced the clouds' march across the lake, listening to the thunder that reverberated overhead. They spoke in whispers, each gazing with hushed awe at the horizon. Rather than abating, the storm seemed to worsen as evening approached and they decided to spend the night in the barn. Arthur arranged several bales together like a nest, and Evelyn lay down among them to nurse the child. Feeling out of place, Gabe and Albra moved to the other side of the loft. Lying in the hay, they spoke in quiet tones, staring at each other in the fading light. As night descended, they became lost to each other, except in the sudden flashes of lightening that broke open the darkness.

Toward dawn, Albra woke just as the rain began to subside. Drawing away from his touch, she went quietly to the corner, waiting as the room filled with light so that she could paint him whole, take him into herself, letting him flow through her veins and into the artery of her brush. As he began to appear on the canvas, she could barely feel the hollow in her chest, now full at last from suffering. And in its fullness there sprang a sense of delicate hope that she had not felt before. In that moment, she knew she would never be this young again.

For Gabe, the touch of her body seemed to connect the world of dreams with the one he woke to, as though he had been born to her in sleep. He saw her now in the first light of dawn, her eyes drawing him out from the earth he knew so well, her fingers brushing back the dirt and all that buried him until he emerged whole into the morning light. As the sun filled the loft, both of them grew very still, listening to the distant waves washing the earth clean.